W9-BML-958

ASLEEP IN THE SUN

Books by Adolfo Bioy Casares
THE INVENTION OF MOREL
PLAN FOR ESCAPE
DIARY OF THE WAR OF THE PIG
ASLEEP IN THE SUN

(with Jorge Luis Borges)
EXTRAORDINARY TALES
CHRONICLES OF BUSTOS DOMECQ

ASLEEP IN THE SUN

by

Adolfo Bioy Casares

translated by Suzanne Jill Levine

PERSEA BOOKS
NEW YORK

Portions of this work first appeared in *Mississippi Review 20*.

International Standard Book Number: 0-89255-030-9
Library of Congress Catalog Card Number: 77-91846
Printed in the United States of America

First Edition

The publisher wishes to thank the Center for Inter-American Relations for their help in making this publication possible.

ASLEEP IN THE SUN

PART ONE

by

Lucio Bordenave

I

This is the third time I'm writing to you. In case they
don't let me finish, I put the first letter in a place I know.
If I want, I can pick it up tomorrow. It's so short and I
wrote it in such a hurry that not even I understand it. I
sent the second one, which isn't much better, with a mes-
senger by the name of Paula. As you haven't given any
signs of life, I'm not going to persist with more useless letters, which might turn you against me. I'm going to tell
you my story from the beginning and I'll try to be clear,
because I need you to understand and to believe me. A
lack of tranquility is the reason for all the crossed-out
words. Every few minutes I get up and put my ear to the
door.

Maybe you wonder: "Why doesn't Bordenave send his
file to a lawyer?" I've seen Mr. Rivaroli only once, but I've
known Fats Picardo (I should be telling you!) for ages. A
lawyer who uses Fats as a front man in the numbers pool
doesn't seem trustworthy. Or maybe you wonder: "Why
does he send the file to me?" If you argue that we're not
friends, you're right, but I also ask you to please put
yourself in my place and tell me to whom I could send it.
After mentally reviewing my friends—leaving out Aldini,
because he's all puffed up with rheumatism—I chose the

11

one who never was. Old Ceferina pontificates: "All of us in the alley live in one big house." By that she means that we all know each other.

Maybe you don't even remember how the argument began.

When the pavement came, in '51 or '52, it was as if they knocked down a fence and opened our alley to the people outside. It was remarkable how long it took us to convince ourselves of the change. You yourself, one Sunday during siesta, applauded the grocer's daughter when she monkeyed around on her bike, as if she was in her own backyard, and you got angry at me because I shouted at the child. I don't blame you if you were quicker to get angry and insulting than to see the automobile that almost ran her over. I stood looking at you like a fool, waiting for an explanation. Perhaps you didn't feel like coming up to me and explaining, or perhaps you thought that the most reasonable thing was for us to resign ourselves to a misunderstanding so often renewed that it was already part of our destiny. Because in reality the matter of the grocer's daughter was not our first disagreement. It was the same old tune.

Ever since we were kids, you and the whole gang would run after me, whenever you remembered to. One afternoon, Fats Picardo, the oldest of the group (if we don't include lame Aldini, who was first fiddle and who more than one Sunday took us to the bleachers at Atlanta), saw me with a tie on when I was coming back from my uncle Miguel's wedding, and he almost strangled me when he fixed my knot. Another time you called me conceited. I forgave you because I guessed that you were offending me only to please the others, knowing that it was a lie. Years later, a doctor who was taking care of the missus explained to me that you and the gang never forgave me my cottage with the red gravel garden and old Ceferina, who took care of me like a nanny and defended me from

12

Picardo. Complicated explanations like that aren't convincing.

Perhaps the strangest consequence of the argument over the grocer's daughter was the idea I'd gotten into my head at the time, and of which I soon became convinced, that you and I had reached an agreement to maintain what I called the distance between us.

I'm getting to the day of my marriage to Diana. I wonder what you thought when you received the invitation. Perhaps you thought you saw a maneuver to break that gentleman's agreement. My intention was, on the contrary, to show the greatest respect and consideration for our misunderstanding.

One afternoon, some time ago, I was talking with Ceferina in the doorway while she threw a pail of water over the sidewalk. I remember that you walked down the middle of the alley and didn't even look at us.

"Are you two going to keep up the fight until Judgment Day?" asked Ceferina with that voice that resounds in her palate.

"It's destiny."

"It's the alley," she answered and her words have not faded from my mind. "An alley is a neighborhood within a neighborhood. In our loneliness the neighborhood gives us company, but it also gives occasion to clashes which provoke or revive hatred."

I dared to contradict her.

"Not so much hatred," I said to her, "Misunderstandings."

Doña Ceferina is a relative, on the Orellana side, who came down from the provinces in my parents' days; when my mother passed away, she never left our side, she was housekeeper, nanny, the true pillar of our household. In the neighborhood they call her the Boss. What they don't know is that this lady, so as not to be less than many who look down upon her, read all the books at the bookstand

13

in Saavedra Park and almost all those in the Basilio Center for Spiritualism in Chas Quarter, which is closer by.

II

I know that some people said I wasn't lucky in marriage. Outsiders would do better not to talk about private affairs, because they're generally wrong. But who would dare tell the neighbors and the family: you are outsiders.

The missus' character is a bit difficult. Diana does not forgive any sort of neglect, nor does she understand it, and if I come home with a special gift she asks me, "To forgive you for what?" She's entirely distrustful and bickers constantly. Any good news makes her sad, because it means that some bad news will come to make up for it.

Neither am I going to deny that on more than one occasion the missus and I have had a disagreement and that one night—I'm afraid the whole alley must have heard the racket—with the intention of seriously leaving I went as far as Incas Street to wait for the bus, which luckily was late and gave me time to think things over. Probably many marriages are familiar with such afflictions. It's modern life, the speed. I know I can tell you that bitter moments and differences did not succeed in separating us.

I'm amazed at the way people loathe pity. By their manner of speaking you take for granted that they're made of steel. When I see her grieving for the things she does when she's not herself, I feel true pity for the missus and, in turn, the missus feels sorry for me when I am upset because of her. Believe me, people think they're

14

made of steel but when it hurts, they soften up. In this matter Ceferina is just like the rest. For her, in pity, there is only weakness and contempt.

Ceferina, who loves me like a son, never fully accepted the missus. In an effort to understand that ill will, I came to suspect that Ceferina would show the same disposition toward any women who came near me. When I expressed this thought to her, Diana answered, "The same goes for me."

People love nobody as much as they do their hatred. I'll admit to you that on more than one occasion, between those two basically good women, I felt abandoned and alone. A good thing that as a last resort I could always take refuge in my watchmaking shop.

I'm going to give you proof that Ceferina's ill will toward Diana was, within the family circle, a public and notorious fact. One morning Ceferina appeared with the newspaper and pointed out to us a small notice which more or less said: *Tragic costume ball in Paso del Molino. Man did not mistrust the masquerader at his side because he thought she was his wife. She was the murderer.* We were so touchy that this item was enough to get us into a fight. Diana, you won't believe this, took the hint, I sided with her, and the old lady—this is pure madness — assumed the air of someone saying *take that,* as if she had read something that compromised the missus or at least all wives. It took me more than fourteen hours to find out that the man at the ball had not been killed by his wife. I didn't want to explain this point to the women, for fear of renewing the argument.

One thing I learned: it is not true that people understand each other by talking. I'll give you as an example a situation that has been repeated more times than you can shake a stick at. I see the missus depressed or sulking and, naturally, I get sad. After a while she asks, "Why are you sad?"

"Because I thought you weren't happy."

"I'm okay now."

I sure feel like telling her that it's not the same with me, that I can't move so quickly from sadness to joy. Perhaps, thinking that I'm being affectionate, I add, "If you don't want to make me sad, don't you ever be sad."

You should see how angry she gets.

"Then don't come to me with the story that it's me you're worried about," she shouts at me as if I were deaf. "What I feel, you don't care about. The master wants his wife to be okay, so that she'll leave him in peace. He's very interested in himself and doesn't want to be bothered. Besides, he's conceited."

"Don't get angry, you'll get a sore on your lip," I say to her, because she's always been prone to get those little sores that bother and irritate her.

She answers me, "Are you afraid you'll catch it?"

I'm not telling you this to speak badly of the missus. Perhaps I'm telling it against myself. When I listen to Diana, I think she's right, although at moments I have doubts. If by chance, then, she gets into her most typical position—cuddled up in an armchair, hugging one leg, with her face resting on her knee, gazing into empty space —I no longer have doubts, I'm in rapture and I beg her to forgive me. I'm mad about her shape and her size, her rosy complexion, her blond hair, her delicate hands, her smell, and above all, her incomparable eyes. Maybe you'll call me a slave; to each his own.

Neighbors aren't slow to argue that someone's wife is lazy or bad-tempered or shiftless, but they don't stop to find out what's the matter with her. Diana, it is proven, suffers for being childless. A doctor explained this to me and it was confirmed by a really sharp-witted lady doctor. When Martincito, my sister-in-law's son, an insufferable little boy, comes to spend a few days with us, the missus

16

goes crazy over him, you wouldn't recognize her, she's a happy woman.

As with so many childless wives, she is strongly attracted to animals. The opportunity of confirming this came along some time ago.

III

Since I lost the bank job I've been getting by on the watchmaking shop. I learned the trade out of pure pleasure, as some learn about radios, photography, or some other sport. I can't complain about a shortage of work. As Don Martin says, as long as people can avoid going downtown they'll risk it with the neighborhood watchmaker.

I'll tell you things as they happened. During the bank employees' strike, Diana's nerves and her tendency to be unhappy in general got the best of her. During the first days, in front of the family and also neighbors and strangers, she scolded me for a supposed lack of nerve and solidarity, but when they locked me up in the first precinct for a whole day and night that seemed like a year to me, and especially when they fired me from the bank, she started to say that to pull the chestnuts out of the fire the trade union bosses always counted on the fools. The poor thing went through a tough moment; I don't think there would have been a way of soothing her then. When I told her that I could get by on the clocks, she wanted me to work in a big used-car showroom, right on Lacarra Avenue. She went with me to talk to the manager, a gentleman who seemed tired, and some young boys, who appeared to be the ones in charge there. Diana got

17

seriously angry because I refused to work with these people. Back home the argument lasted a week, until the police broke into the Lacarra locale and there appeared in the newspapers photographs of the manager and the boys, who turned out to be a famous gang.

In any case the missus stood firm in her opposition to the watchmaking shop. I'd better not don the magnifying glass in her presence, because that gesture inexplicably irritates her. I remember that one afternoon she said to me, "There's no getting away from it. I have a grudge against clocks!"

"Tell me why."

"Because they're little and full of little wheels and windings. Someday I'm going to go into your shop and make the biggest mess of the century, even if we'll have to move to the other side of the city."

I said, to make friends with her, "Admit that you like cuckoo clocks."

She smiled because she was surely imagining the little house and little bird, and she answered in a better mood. "They almost never bring you a cuckoo clock. Instead they always come with those mammoth grandfather clocks. The chimes are something that get on my nerves."

As Ceferina pontificates, everyone has his own tastes and his own opinions. Even though one doesn't always understand them, one should accept them.

"The rumor went around that I have a knack for grandfather clocks. Even from the North Quarter they bring them."

"Let's move to the North Quarter."

I tried to discourage her.

"Don't you know that it's the focal point of grandfather clocks?" I said to her.

"Yes, but it is the North Quarter," she answered pensively.

You can't deny that she has Irala blood. In the "royal

family," as Ceferina calls them, they go all out to cut a figure in society and rub shoulders with the right people.

For me, the idea of moving was always upsetting. I feel attached to the house, to the alley, to the neighborhood. Life has now taught me that love for things, like all unrequited love, takes its toll in the long run. Why didn't I listen to the missus' plea? If I had gone away in time, now we would be free. With resentment and with distrust, I picture the neighborhood, as if these rows of houses that I know by heart had turned into the walls of a prison where the missus and I are condemned to a destiny worse than death. Until recently we lived happily. I insisted upon staying and, as you see, now it is too late to escape.

IV

Last August we met a Mr. Standle, a teacher in the dog school on Estomba Street. I'll bet you've seen him more than once in the neighborhood, always with a different dog, that always walks as if waiting for orders and that doesn't even growl for fear of making him angry. Try to remember: a big guy in a trench coat, blond, straight as a broomstick, kind of square because of his broad shoulders, a shaven face, small, gray eyes that don't blink, I swear, even if the next guy is squirming and screaming. In the alley there are all sorts of rumors going around about that guy: that he came as a lion tamer with the Sarrasini Circus, that he was a hero in the last war, a maker of soap with fat from God knows what bones, and an indisputable ace spy who transmitted by radio, from a villa in Ramos, instructions to a fleet of submarines which was preparing an invasion of the country. To all this add, please, the afternoon when Aldini stood up as well as he could from the little bench where he'd take the fresh air with his dog, that seems to be as old and rheumatic as him, grabbed me by the arm, took me aside as if there were people nearby—but on the sidewalk there was only us and the dog—and blew into my ear, "He's a Teutonic knight."

V

Another afternoon, while we were sipping our *maté*, Diana commented to Ceferina, "I'll bet he doesn't even remember."

She moved her head in my direction. I sat looking at her with my mouth open, because at first I didn't remember that Sunday was my birthday.

Diana punctually observes all kinds of birthdays, anniversaries, Mother's, Grandfather's, and whatever other Day occurs to the calendar or to whoever runs these things, so that she doesn't tolerate any neglect of those matters. If the forgotten date would have been her own birthday or my father-in-law, Don Martín Irala's, or the anniversary of our marriage, I would do better to exile myself from the alley, because for me there would be no pardon.

"Invite only the family," I begged her.

At our house, the family is the missus'

As it was my birthday she finally gave in and we celebrated it just among us. Believe me, it took a lot of convincing. She's very fond of parties.

So on the night of my birthday, Don Martín came, Adriana María, my sister-in-law, her son Martincito and —by what right I wonder?—the German, Standle.

You must have seen Don Martín in the garden with the

hoe and sprinkler. He's very fond of flowers and all kinds of vegetables. You most probably took him for one of those gardeners-by-the-hour. If that's true, my father-in-law had better not find out. Everyone in the family is afflicted with the pride of their blood ever since a specialist, who for two or three dollars concocted genealogies at a stand in the Cattle Fair, told them that they are direct descendants of an Irala who had been eaten by the Indians. Don Martín is a stout man, rather short, bald, with blue eyes, and known for his fits of bad temper. As soon as he arrived he claimed my wool slippers. I can't refuse him, believe me, because they got to be second nature to him; but when I see him with the slippers on I feel angry at him. You might think that a person who appropriates one's slippers, even if it's only for awhile, does it as a pledge of some feeling of friendship. Don Martín doesn't share that opinion and, if he speaks to me, it's to bark at me. I must admit that on my birthday night (like everyone else, except me) he was happy. It was the cider. And also, of course, the meal: abundant, fresh, the best quality, prepared to a T. At our house there may be lots of failings, but not as far as eating is concerned.

Allow me to duly clarify the point: Diana always considered herself a good hand in the kitchen. A merit of recognized weight in the household. Her little Indian puddings are justly famous in the immediate family and even among relatives.

When the sports news was over, Don Martín turned off the television. Martincito, who bellows as if he were imitating a boy bellowing, demanded it be turned on again. Don Martín, with amazing calm, took off the right slipper and gave him a kick. Martincito screamed. Diana protected him, spoiled him; she goes all out for him. Don Martín thundered, "Time to eat."

"Guess the surprise?" Diana asked.

21

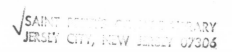

Right away they all broke into an unmistakable uproar. Even Ceferina, who's such a relentless fighter, participated in that small show, which furthermore was sincere. Diana puts as much pride as she does good will into her work, so that she's not going to admit her Indian puddings come out bad or are indigestible.

At our house, every once in a while, one can hear the chimes of some wall clock that's been put on observation. Nobody that I know of is irritated by the frequent but harmonious ringing of bells; nobody except Diana or Don Martín. When a cuckoo clock went off, Don Martín faced me squarely and shouted, "That bird better shut up because I'm going to wring his neck."

"Oh Papa," Diana protested, "I can't stand clocks either, but the cuckoo is what I call sweet. Wouldn't you like to live in his little house? I would."

"To me the most infuriating clocks are the cuckoos," said Don Martín, already somewhat calmed down by Diana.

Like me, he's crazy about her.

Martincito ate in the most disgusting manner. He left traces of his sticky hands all over the house.

"The children of our fellowmen are angels disguised as devils," commented Ceferina in that resounding voice of hers. "God sends them to try our patience."

I admit that at no moment of the night did I feel happy. I mean really happy. Perhaps I was ill-disposed by a premonition, because ever since I can remember, I regard birthdays, Christmas, and New Year's with mistrust. I try to hide it so as not to ruin celebrations which the missus so much appreciates, but most probably I worry and am in a bad mood. And with reason: the worst things happened to me on those dates.

Let me clarify that, until lately, the worst things had been quarrels with Diana and fits of jealousy for offenses that existed only in my imagination.

You'll probably say the missus is right, you'll probably say that I'm self-centered, that I never tire of explaining what I feel.

In the letter Nurse Paula brought you, I didn't give any details. After reading it, not even I was convinced. I thought it was logical, then, that you hadn't answered. In this account, however, I'm explaining everything, even my weaknesses and my eccentricities, so that you'll see how I am and know me. I want to believe that you will think you can definitely trust me.

VI

That night of my birthday, Professor Standle, talking about dogs, cornered everybody's attention. It was remarkable how those present became interested not only in dog training, but in the school's organization. I am the first—if the professor is not lying—to recognize the school's results, and I won't deny that for the space of one or two minutes those animal stories bewitched me. While others spoke of the advantages and disadvantages of the training collar, I let myself be carried away by pure fantasy and in my heart of hearts I wondered if those who denied that dogs had souls were in the right. As the professor says, between their intelligence and ours there is only a difference of degree; but I'm not sure that difference always exists. Some pupils of the school develop —if I can rely on the German's accounts—just like honest-to-God human beings.

Mr. Standle's voice, the most humdrum and solemn buzz that one can ask for, awakened me from my reveries. Although I don't know why, I find that voice unpleasant. The man expounded, "We educate, sell, bathe them, cut their hair, and even set up the nicest beauty salon for luxury pooches."

The missus asked, "Are there people who take their dogs to school, like others send their children? The poor things, do they cry the first day?"

"My school trains watchdogs," Standle gravely answered.

"Let's take one thing at a time," said Don Martín. "Why all the science needed for that? With a collar and a chain, I can turn even you into a watchdog."

"The school takes one step further," replied Standle.

My father-in-law, usually so sullen, attempted to maintain a principle of authority, but not with conviction. In reality, he listened enraptured and when the cuckoo clock went off he apparently didn't hear it. Why deny it? They were all hanging on the professor's words, except old Ceferina, who, out of stubborn resentment toward the missus and her family, remained aloof and beneath a scornful smile hid her lively interest.

Goodness knows why I felt abandoned and sad. A good thing Adriana María, my sister-in-law—she looks like the missus, a dark-haired version—took pity on me and from time to time asked if I didn't want another glass of cider.

The professor continued.

"We are not simply returning to the master a domesticated animal. We are returning a high fidelity companion."

When I heard these boring words I didn't even remotely suspect their terrible consequences. Believe you me, they affected the missus' mind. I'm not being an alarmist. You must know, because everyone in the alley knows, that even before she was married Diana had been put in a sanatorium at least twice. I'll admit that at the beginning of the conversation she got on to the subject of dogs with apparent calm, speaking in a low voice, perfectly fine, like someone who was controlling herself.

"In a house with a garden," she remarked pensively, "it's a good idea to have a dog."

"Very much so," pronounced the German.

I didn't agree but neither did I disagree. I greatly fear that this moderation on my part encouraged the missus. In the wrong direction, of course.

Various aspects of the same matter (dogs, the school) nurtured the conversation until very late.

Suddenly, my father-in-law declared, "If I go home late, I won't get to sleep. A good deal you care. But I do."

Of course I didn't care if my father-in-law slept or not, but with incredible zest I defended myself against that accusation of indifference which I repeatedly qualified as unfair. Adriana María's interpretation of my protest made me smile.

"The poor birthday boy!" she said affectionately. "He's so sleepy he's dropping off and he wants us to leave him in peace."

I was not sleepy (I only wanted them to leave), but I thought it better not to explain.

Although the conversation continued, I considered their departure imminent, because we had stood up. At the last minute there were delays. Don Martín had to go to the bathroom and afterward he turned the house upside down because he couldn't find his scarf. Adriana María, who had been in such a hurry and who, suffocating with laughter, pointed to me with her finger and repeated, "The poor thing can't take any more," engaged in God knows what long explanations with Ceferina, who looked down at her from on high. Don Martín, if I didn't look in time, would have taken my slippers. Useless to clarify that the kid didn't have the civility to bring his grandfather's high-buttoned shoes. After the family's departure, the professor was reserving an unpleasant surprise for me. He came back into the house with us.

VII

Believe you me, the nightmare we are still living began that very night. Without caring about what I thought, Professor Standle pushed the missus into her obsession with dogs. I couldn't complain for fear that she would take his side and be on her guard against me.

The situation became more intolerable, I mean the fact that the professor resorted to tasteless explanations, which couldn't possibly interest any lady.

"The last word in watchdogs is the bitch," he stated, as if he were revealing a profound truth. "Thieves will put a bitch in heat in front of your best male dog and you can forget about your watchdog. On the other hand, a bitch is always faithful."

I don't know why these words provoked in the missus a kind of uncontrollable laughter, which seemed pitiful and never-ending.

We talked about dogs until the fellow — at an hour that makes one feel guilty for being awake — said he was leaving. If I didn't stand firm, we would have accompanied him to the school. In any case, we had to go as far as the street door.

When we came back in, the house seemed untidy, stale with cigarette smoke, and sad. Diana dropped into an armchair, cuddled up, hugging one leg, leaned her face against her knee, and stared into space. Seeing her that way I said to myself, I swear, I couldn't live without her. Also, stimulated by enthusiasm, I conceived truly extraordinary thoughts and fell to asking myself, What is Diana to me? Her soul? Her body? I love her eyes, her face, her hands, the smell of her hands and her hair. Ceferina assures me that God will punish me for such thoughts. I don't believe there's another woman on earth with such beautiful eyes. I never tire of admiring them. I imagine dawns like grottos of water and I build up hopes that I will discover in their depths Diana's true soul. A wonderful soul, like her eyes.

Diana herself tore me from these reflections when she started fantasizing and saying that we were going to have a dog that would accompany us and understand us like a close friend. You felt like you were listening to a child. To make it worse, Diana talked so fast that if I didn't hurry to protest, her statements faded into the distance and I had to coax her to retrace her steps so that we could discuss them. Besides, she was so nervous (and I wanted her so much) that, so as not to contradict her, I often didn't put her wise. If I had tried to, God help me. She's very hard when she gets angry and, believe you me, she won't make up until you've crawled to her feet and begged forgiveness until Doomsday. I only dared to remark, "Ceferina says there's something monstrous and very sad about animals."

"When I was little I wanted to have a zoo," Diana answered.

"Ceferina says that animals, maybe, are people who've been punished with the curse of not being able to talk."

Just imagine the missus. Even in her madness she's quick and has an answer for everything. She asked me, "Didn't you hear what Professor Standle said?"

"I heard too much."

She insisted, unflappable, "About dogs that talk."

"Frankly, I missed that nonsense."

"You were uncorking a bottle of cider. He told us that another professor, a countryman of his, taught a dog to pronounce three words in perfect German."

"What kind of dog?" I asked, like an idiot.

"I remember the word 'Eberfeld.' I can't say whether it's the breed or the city where they lived or the professor's name."

I had many weak moments that night and I'm still paying for them.

VIII

My sorrow accompanied me all night long. Sad thoughts kept me from sleeping and, when I heard the cock Aldini has in his backyard, I said to myself that the next day I was going to be tired and that my hands would shake while I worked. Finally, I fell asleep to dream that I lost Diana, I think on Avenida de Mayo, where we had met Aldini who said, "Let me separate you two for a moment, to tell you a completely insignificant secret." Very smilingly he made the gesture of separating us and immediately pointed his finger at me. Just then the carnival parade flowed into the avenue and dragged Diana away with it. I saw her disappear among the masqueraders disguised as animals who passed by endlessly, their bodies striped with colors like zebras or snakes, and with dog heads of painted cardboard that were totally expressionless. You won't believe me: still asleep, I asked myself if my dream was really about what happened or a premonition of what was going to happen. You won't believe me either if I tell you that, awake, I was still in the nightmare.

Around that time the missus no longer stayed home; she spent the whole damn day at the school, without deciding on any pet. An inability to make decisions which, as Standle himself commented one evening, gives one food for thought. I waited for her impatiently and kept having absurd wild thoughts: that something had happened to her, that she wasn't going to come back. There were days when we ate dinner late because the missus didn't come home, and others when Ceferina and I after eating played goldfish, when we didn't play hearts, to pass the time. The sounds of the night were enough reason for me to every once in a while stick my head out the door. Ceferina would then add, her long face now frequently full of anger and contempt, words mumbled under her breath which could be heard perfectly.

"The young master is worried. His little wife hasn't come home. He might lose her yet."

The general intention and tone were always the same. Sometimes I couldn't stand it and in a voice that pretended to be indifferent I'd say, "I'm going out for a walk."

If you think I'm not the proper age to be asking permission, you're right. It's very easy to tell the next man how to run his life, but everyone does the best he can. What do you suggest? That I throw Ceferina out? All things considered, it would be as if I were throwing my own late mother out. Should I shout at her? I don't like to spend my life shouting. Ceferina, with her angry face and shining eyes, clearly shows her disapproval. For me that disapproval, how should I say, is something real, that's in my way, like the corner of a table. Don't ask me to bump against it each time I go past it, because I prefer to live in peace and go around it. That bit about living in peace is a manner of speaking.

As I was saying, if I became uneasy, with the pretext of getting some fresh air I'd go out, choose the least lighted spot, lean against the fence, and wait. I'd wait with anguish in my soul, because Diana would take longer than expected, but also because the neighbors were constantly appearing; they live to catch one by surprise so that they can then spread their comments all over the alley.

One night Picardo came right up to me, as if he knew where he was going to find me and, without bothering about excuses or extenuating circumstances, he said, "I think he gave her something. Rivaroli, a friend I'm going to introduce you to, explained that a couple of pills in her coffee is enough. When he's tired of keeping her as a slave, he sells her to the white slave traders in Central America."

Another night Aldini himself, who according to Ceferina is losing his eyesight, with the excuse of taking the dog out (or rather dragging him out, because poor Naughty Boy, before he knows it, starts trembling and then collapses), as I was saying, with the excuse of taking the dog out, walked up to where I was—I swear, the darkest spot—and said to me, "Please don't listen to Picardo. Nowadays drugs are the explanation for every thing. Take my word, they exaggerate."

Neither you nor I are going to believe that little story about the pills in her coffee. I admit, however, that when Diana would finally come home, she'd have dog hairs stuck all over her dress. What's more, she smelled of dogs. She'd talk about dogs and about the German (I couldn't make out when she was referring to them and when to him), she talked at full speed, as if an itch were driving her crazy and, because the night wasn't long enough to discuss the merits and shortcomings of bloodhounds, sheepdogs, and mastiffs, we'd continue the debate in the morning, until the missus would take to the streets and I would fall asleep over the clocks.

IX

That professor, who could teach Judas a few lessons, telephoned me one afternoon to meet him in Buggy's Bar, which faces Carbajal.

"What's the occasion?" I asked him.

He answered immediately.

"To talk about the missus."

Although I understood, I asked him to clarify.

"Whose missus?"

"Yours."

As you can well understand, I couldn't believe my ears, but I mastered my feelings and answered with disgust.

"Who are you to butt in?"

I was still uttering these words, when my blood froze with fear. Could something have happened to Diana? I'd do better not to waste time.

Professor Standle began to say in a strangely squeaky voice, "Well, you know..."

I flatly interrupted him. "I'll be right there."

I ran down the street. In Buggy's I chose a table from where you could see the entrance at all times, I ordered something, and before they served me I was already wondering if I shouldn't head for the dog school. What made me say, "I'll be right there," and hang up? Perhaps the professor thought that I would go to the school, but if I didn't get there on time, maybe he'd wonder if "there" didn't mean Buggy's and perhaps we'd meet, or miss each other, on the way.

As far as you're concerned, you must be wondering why I'm telling you all this tomfoolery. Since the night of my birthday up until now, except for short intervals of peace, I've lived in a permanent state of confusion. Seen by others, any confused man acts like a clown.

After an endless half-hour—because I finally stayed in the bar—the professor appeared. He came over to the table, asked for a bock beer, took off his trenchcoat, folded it carefully, placed it on the back of a chair, took a seat and, I swear to you, that not until drinking the beer and wiping the foam off his mouth did he say a word. When he spoke, for a moment his face became blurry to me, as if I were having a dizzy spell. This is the first thing I heard.

"You know that the missus is very ill."

"Diana?" I murmured.

"Missus Diana," he corrected me.

"What's the matter with her? Is she sick?"

He answered with extreme scorn. "Don't pretend you don't understand. She's very ill. If we don't act fast, she might reach the point of no return."

"I want her to return."

"You want to close your eyes so as not to see reality," he answered, "but you know what I'm talking about."

"I don't quite understand yet." I tried to make excuses. "There's something there but my head keeps going around in circles."

"We act immediately or you lose the missus for all practical purposes."

"Let's act," I said, and I asked him to explain how.

Then he spoke in a very low voice. "The answer," he said, "is to put her away."

I managed to protest. "Not that..."

He fell back into the squeaky voice and remarked, as if he were satisfied, "The incapacity to make decisions, demonstrated by Missus Diana, who can't decide which pooch she wants, is not usual in people in their right minds."

I think the professor used the words "put away" on purpose. In any case I felt as if I had been hit. Not without reason. Poor Diana, when she remembered the time she spent in the sanatorium, she'd start trembling like a frightened animal, she'd grasp my hands, and, as if she were demanding all my attention and the whole truth, she'd ask, "Now that I'm married, they can't put me away, right?" I'd answer her that no, they couldn't, and I believed what I was telling her.

Standle continued, "Does it seem right to you that the missus spends the whole damn day out of the house?"

"If only it weren't more than the damn day..." I sighed.

"And a good part of the night. Do you sit there waiting for her calmly?"

"No, I don't wait for her calmly."

"While she's in the hospital, your headaches are over."

God forgive me, I said, "Do you think so?"

"Of course," he answered. "If you give me your okay, I'll get in touch with Dr. Reger Samaniego."

"Poor Diana is very nervous," I murmured, and I felt bad, as if I had said something hypocritical.

"Don't tell me," he replied. "Dr. Samaniego will have her back in shape in no time. Want to know something? Sometimes they call him for consultations from downtown! But don't get your hopes up. There might be a hitch."

"A hitch?" I asked anxiously.

"Maybe they won't take her. Not everyone gets into Dr. Reger Samaniego's Psychiatric Institute."

"Is there any way..."

"He has a long waiting list. Also, I don't know how much he charges."

"That doesn't matter," I asserted.

It's not that I'm rich, but I'm not going to think of money when it comes to Diana.

"Don't worry," the professor said.

"No problem," I protested angrily.

"The institute is on Baigorria Street. Right around the corner from here. You can visit her whenever you feel like it. Tomorrow, first thing in the morning, I'll come get her."

I looked at him surprised, though I knew perfectly well that he was real chummy with the doctor, because Friday nights they play chess, in full view of the public, at The Bend, on the corner of Álvarez Thomas and Donado. It's true that I knew all this by hearsay; through one of those great tricks of fate, up until that time I had never set eyes on Dr. Reger Samaniego, with his mummy face.

33

X

Professor Standle stood up, while I hurried to pay so as not to sit there like a chump, and I believe I helped him on with his raincoat, which cost me some effort, since the beast is at least six feet tall. It seems hard to believe, but I thanked him several times, because I still saw him as a friend and protector. It was only because of the difficulty I had finding the words that I didn't say to him, "You can't imagine the load you've taken off my back."

That mood lasted till he went away. Then I felt—I don't know if I'm making myself clear—without support, not at all happy about the decision I had made. God knows, maybe Standle had seemed to be my protector, because he didn't let me open my mouth to express my doubts. I think I felt afraid, as if I set in motion an unpredictable calamity. I walked around the neighborhood a bit, so as not to get home too soon, especially so as not to go home with that sorrowful face and that stiffness around my jaws that kept me from looking like I was in a good mood or at least indifferent. Also, I wanted to think things over because I didn't know what to say to Diana.

Suddenly I shouted, "I can't do that to her." I couldn't make deals with a stranger, behind her back, to put her away. I would never forgive myself; she, believe me, wouldn't either. Wild plans came to my mind. To suggest to her that very night that we spend a week at a resort on the Tigre delta (it wasn't the right season) or that we head for Mar del Plata or Montevideo to try our luck at the Casino.

Of course if Diana asked me, "Why don't we wait till tomorrow morning, are we leaving in the middle of the night as if we were escaping?" I wouldn't have an answer.

I don't remember if I told you that the missus is very brave. Of course she had bad memories of the sanatorium where they put her away when she was single and the poor thing counted on me also to defend her from any doctor or nurse who came near the house, but if she would have suspected that I was suggesting escape, apart from feeling disappointed and even despising me, nothing would have induced her to follow me, even if she knew they were coming for her the following morning. How different people are: until that moment I hadn't stopped to consider the possibility that someone would interpret my plans as an attempt to escape. My only worry had been to save the missus.

It's true that if you push me a little I'll admit that I made a deal to give the missus away so that I wouldn't make a bad impression in the conversation. I will add, if you wish, something even worse. When the professor was out of sight, I no longer cared if I made a good or a bad impression and I was amazed at the atrocity I had consented to. Poor Diana, so trusting of her Lucho; at the first opportunity you see how well he defended her. Although she doesn't love me as much as I love her, I'm sure that nobody could make her abandon me like that...The missus' courage and fortitude amaze me and at difficult moments, like the ones I'm going through, they are an example to me.

You can appreciate how wrong those people are who say that I was unlucky in marriage.

There was a surprise for me when I got home. When I turned on the bedroom light, Diana, who was already in bed, pretended to be asleep. I have good reason to say this, because I caught her looking at me with one completely awake eye. In that confusion I went to think things over in the kitchen where Ceferina was cleaning up. If I'm in the midst of a quarrel with the missus, I prefer not to run into her, because she doesn't like Diana.

"What's the matter with her?" she asked, while she made me some *maté*.

As if I didn't understand, I asked, "With whom?"

"Who's it going to be? Your missus. She's very strange. She can't fool me; she's up to something."

XI

The next morning, when the professor came, Diana was sleeping or pretending to be asleep. It's true that I myself — though I hadn't slept a wink all night — was caught by surprise when the fellow appeared. It sure must have been early, since Aldini's cock hadn't even crowed yet.

My performance on the occasion left something to be desired, because I lost my head. I think that men years ago were much more manly. What a disgrace. I asked that Johnny-come-lately, "What should I do?"

With his invariable calm he answered, "Tell her I've come to get her."

That's what I did and, you should see, without asking for any explanations the missus ran to freshen up and dress. I thought that we'd be awhile, because with things like that women take more time than you expect. I was wrong; after a few minutes she came out looking ravishing and with her overnight bag in hand. I suspect that she had everything ready before going to bed.

Now I'm starting to get wise to the fact that maybe the professor talked her into it the evening before, at the school. God knows what lies he told her. Seeing how she'd been fooled made me feel sorry for her and hate the professor. On this point I was unfair, because the one to blame was myself; I'd promised to protect the missus and I got involved in the treachery. Diana kissed me and like a child, or rather like a puppy, followed Standle.

Ceferina said, "The house seems as empty as if they'd taken the furniture away."

Her voice, which always resounds on her palate, then resounded in the room as well. Perhaps the old woman spoke maliciously, but she expressed what I felt.

After a while she began to be annoying. She was too attentive and affectionate, she carried her good humor to notable extremes of vulgarity, and even hummed the tango "Victory." I wondered at the fact that a person who loves us can increase our unhappiness. I went into the shop to work on the clocks.

XII

We had just sat down at the table, old Ceferina very lively and with a great appetite, me with my throat choked up so that not even water would pass through, when the telephone rang. I answered like a shot, because I thought it was Diana calling me to come get her. It was Don Martín, my father-in-law.

As the poor guy doesn't hear too well, at first he simply thought that his daughter was not at home. When it had gotten through to him that we'd put her away, I swear I was afraid on the telephone. Apart from the fact that my father-in-law gets angry quickly and frightens people with his bad temper, by then the fact that I had put Diana away had taken on, even for me, the nature of an atrocity. I said to myself that before Don Martín could visit us, I would drag Diana home by the arm.

"I'm off," I announced.

"Without eating?" asked Ceferina, alarmed.

"I'm going right this minute."

"If you don't eat, you're going to get weak," she complained. "Why do you let the old man get you all steamed up?"

That got me angry and I answered, "And why do you listen to conversations that are none of your business?"

"So he just got you all steamed up. Did he order you to fetch his little daughter? A good thing that when you come back at least you'll eat well, because she's going to be doing the cooking for you."

These fights with the old woman upset me. Without saying a word, I went out.

I hadn't reached the corner when Fats Picardo crossed my path. There was the proof: the times when you're most distressed you bump into a clown like Picardo and the things that happen to you no longer seem real, but rather like a dream. In spite of that, things don't improve. You're just as troubled, but less firmly grounded.

"Where are you going?" he asked.

When he speaks, the way Picardo moves his Adam's apple is very noticeable.

"I have things to do," I said.

He eyed me persistently, barely hiding his curiosity. It's amazing to think that we once considered him a kind of bully, but now he's not only the biggest fool in the neighborhood, but also the skinniest.

"We saw your missus this morning," he said. "She went out early."

"What's the matter with that?" I asked.

I don't know why I remember a detail of that moment: without wanting to, I noticed the poorly shaven hairs on his Adam's apple.

"Are you going to get her?" he asked.

"What makes you think that?" I answered without thinking.

He said, "You should try your luck at the numbers."

"Leave me alone."

"I'm taking bets. This lawyer who comes to The Bend once in a while knew that we have a telephone so he appointed me his agent. I start work next week." He paused and added with unexpected poise, "I'd like you to be one of my customers."

I was about to tell him that that work wasn't for fools, but I wanted to get rid of him, so I promised, "I'll be your customer if you stay right here."

I remember the meeting with Picardo to the smallest detail. In fact, I remember all that happened after my horrible birthday night as if it were taking place right before my eyes. One forgets a dream; but never a nightmare like this.

XIII

The dog school occupies the spacious but bumpy lot which, when we were kids, had been the place of Galache's orchard and chicken yard. The building, as the German calls it, is the old lodge, only now it's older, with its dried-up wood — since Galache's times it hadn't been given what you call a paint job — and with rotten, unnailed boards here and there. I was always amazed that the orchard produced such fragrant peaches, because the whole place was covered with the smell of chickens. Now, it smells of dogs.

I don't know why I became so suspicious as I got close to it. You'll say, "You're afraid of dogs." Believe me, that's not it. It was a fantasy: I imagined that by entering without warning I would discover a secret that would bring me sorrow. I thought, Things should be open and aboveboard. I'm telling you this detail because it shows how my mind was working; before knowing a thing, as if I had forebodings of the trials they'd put me through, I was flying a bit off the handle. I thought, Things should be open and aboveboard, and I started calling out. After a while the professor came out. He didn't seem happy about my visit.

When I came into his office he asked me, "Would you like some coffee?"

I was going to say no, to state my complaint at once; but I know myself, I know that when I'm nervous I'm not worth a thing, so I said yes, to gain time and to see if I could calm down. The German left the room.

I'm not the kind that brags about predicting events, but I wonder why I seemed, from the very beginning, so upset. It's true that giving one's missus, more or less through deceit, over to an insane asylum is enough to disturb any man. I said to myself, I'm frightened because of what I did, but I swear, I suspected that behind that there was something even worse.

There was no air in the little room. On the walls there were pictures of dogs, framed as if they were people, and a watercolor which showed a battleship on whose prow I could make out the word "Tirpitz." The professor's desk, the kind that has a sliding, wavy lid like a shutter, was stocked with yellowish papers. He pushed them aside a little to put down his coffee mug, a soup spoon, and a porcelain sugar bowl. On the floor, next to the swivel chair, there was an open red, white, and blue tin of Bay Biscuits. It was a big tin, the kind you see behind counters.

Now I'm thinking that I was looking at those things as if they were alive.

He brought me the coffee in a teacup.

"You'll have to excuse me," he said. "Here there are no two cups that are alike and there's no spoon. Besides, maybe you don't like coffee."

I looked at him, surprised.

"Because it's not coffee," he explained. "Coffee is bad, too stimulating. Cereal is good. Would you like some sugar?"

XIV

Isn't it something: the cereal gave me a basis to overcome my fears.

"It's disgusting, but it doesn't matter." I pushed aside
the teacup. "It doesn't matter."

"I don't understand," he said gravely.

"I'm thinking about something entirely different."

"You're thinking about the missus."

Then I was the one who was caught off guard. I asked
him, "How do you know?"

Did he guess out of pure shrewdness, or was I so
disturbed that without realizing it I made my thoughts
perfectly clear? His answer didn't clarify anything.

"Because you regret what you did."

"There's no cause to be satisfied." I cautioned him.
"You've done some harm here. People who do harm to
others should undo it."

He went into a long speech in a reasonable tone which
turned out to be insolent and even ridiculous when his
voice, usually thick and low, started squeaking. In short,
he harped on the dangers of her illness and the comforts
of the institute.

"The way you make it sound one would think that you
put her into a first-class hotel. A palace."

"It's as good as a palace."

He added a word which sounded like *kestle* or
something like that. Not understanding helped me get
angry.

"You take my missus out of there," I shouted. "You
take her out."

There was a very long silence.

"Take out, take out," he finally answered while he
knocked me on the forehead with the tip of his forefinger,

hard as steel. "I'll take that idea out of your head, that's what I'll do."

I looked at him. He's huge, a regular wardrobe dressed as a person.

"If the missus has any complaints when she comes back, I'll make you responsible."

I tried to seem menacing, but my words came out conciliatory. Besides, when I said, "when she comes back," I was afraid of getting my hopes up and I ended up looking rather desperate.

"If you take her out," he answered, "you're the responsible one. I wouldn't play that dirty trick on Missus Diana. I don't do that kind of thing."

I don't know why I got even madder at him for the way he said, "I don't do that kind of thing." We argued a while. Finally, like a little boy on the verge of tears, I confided, "I have the feeling that this time I've lost her forever."

I hated myself for showing so much weakness. Standle advised me, "If you insist, why don't you speak directly with Dr. Reger Samaniego?"

"No, no," I said, defending myself.

"The smartest thing is for you to go back home. Now."

I walked out like a sleepwalker. I hadn't reached the wire fence, when I was alarmed by a thought. Maybe the man's confused, I said to myself, and rapidly started thinking. He doesn't know that he beats me in conversations because he's quicker. Maybe he thinks I'm afraid of him. If he believes that, the missus won't have the slightest protection. I did an about-face, went back to the lodge, opened the door an inch, and looked in. The professor again seemed displeased.

"The missus better not have any complaints, because you and that doctor are going to have a hard time of it." Since he opened his mouth and didn't answer, I shouted at him, "If you have something to say, speak."

"No, no," he stammered. "There won't be any complaint."

In one gulp he drank that coffee which was cereal and which must have been lukewarm. I closed the door. I walked away in triumph, but the satisfaction didn't last long. I said to myself, Poor Diana is right. I am miserably involved with my own vanity. For all I know I might be delaying her freedom with all this showing off.

XV

When I got home, Adriana María was already there. I mean she was there to stay, kid and all. Unlike my father-in-law, she was affectionate and congratulated me for my "brave and timely" attitude. She explained, "Papa was always an enemy of insane asylums. When Mommy passed away, he swore that there would no longer be any force in the world capable of putting Diana away. Papa didn't figure on the hubby being that force."

I believe I smiled with satisfaction, since any compliment is soothing to a person who doesn't hear them too often, but my mood changed when I realized I was being congratulated for nothing less than putting Diana away. I protested as much as I could.

"The thing is," Adriana María said, in that little tone of voice people get when they're giving you a complete explanation, "you don't know the tears I've shed on account of Papa's little whim."

"What little whim?"

"Just like I said. He's nuts about Diana."

I answered, "It's not Diana's fault that people love her."

"I agree. You're absolutely right. But you too will agree

that I know my family. I am, how shall I say, familiar with it."

I looked at her surprised and thought, I don't understand. When I am most troubled about the missus, I suddenly discover that my sister-in-law has a sense of humor. A cute little phrase of Adriana María's, which rang out loud and clear, awoke me from these thoughts.

"I look like Mommy, and Diana is the spitting image of the old man."

With a fury that not even a psychoanalyst could explain to me, I immediately answered, "Everyone in the family looks alike, but I love Diana."

"Ever since I was a little girl," she said, "my life has been a struggle. While my friends played with their dolls, I shed tears and struggled. I've always had a struggle."

"How sad."

"Do you really think it's sad?" she anxiously asked. "A free young widow, and I behave in a way that more than one married woman would envy. Did you ever stop to think what my life was like?"

I answered her sincerely.

"Never."

My life is the empty hole that Rodolfo, my husband, left behind when he passed away. I swear by Mommy that no one has filled it until now."

I felt uncomfortable. Perhaps I realized, without needing to think too much, that Adriana María was someone on the outside, ready to butt in where she wasn't wanted and demanding all sorts of attention at a moment when all I asked for was peace and understanding. I hid my disappointment as well as I could and, as the tango says, in search of a fraternal breast, I went off to Ceferina's room, down the hall. At the very door a collision occurred; it wasn't a hard bump since Ceferina was loaded down with pillows and blankets, but it confused me.

Those who love us have a right to hate us from time to time. As if bumping into me had made her happy, she commented, "We're not gaining much, are we?"

Although I knew it was wiser to keep quiet, I asked, "What makes you say that?"

"They've always kept me in this house to make the beds of shameless hussies."

Her voice whistled with rage.

I said, "I'm going to work on my clocks."

As I passed by the bathroom, I think I saw Adriana María in the mirror with her breasts half-uncovered. It's a good thing Ceferina didn't catch her, because we would have had a topic of conversation for quite awhile.

XVI

I threw myself into my work, impelled by a mysterious itch, maybe by the hope that the clocks would occupy my thoughts. As it got closer to dinner time, I figured that if I kept going at the same rate, the repair jobs promised for the end of the month would be ready by the end of the week.

It was the turn of the druggist's Roskopf watch. Whatever the topic of conversation, Don Francisco, as if he were wound up like a clock, always manages to come up with maxims like this: "It's to my credit" or "They don't make machines like this anymore" or, if not that, the one which for him sums up all other praise, "I inherited it from my late father." While I took the watch apart, I thought, So as not to contradict Standle, I let them lock her up in the mental institute. Not in vain does Diana say that husbands, in their eagerness to please the first stranger who comes their way, sacrifice their wives. Don't ask me what was wrong with the Roskopf watch: I worked on that machine with my mind somewhere else entirely.

After a while my thoughts and the clocks themselves became unbearable. I believe that again I thought Diana was right and I even felt a repulsion toward the watchmaker's craft. Why look so closely at such little details? I got up from the bench and walked around the room like a caged animal, until the chimes began to ring. Then I turned off the light and left.

I went into the dining room, which was dark, with the television turned on. Believe me, for a moment I almost couldn't stand the joy: from the back, facing the screen, who do I see? You're right: Diana. I was already running to embrace her, when she must have heard me or guessed my presence, because she turned around. It was Adriana María. I must admit that she looks like the missus; in a darker version, as I already told you, and with noticeable differences of character. Seeing that it wasn't Diana, I felt such a grudge against the woman that without meaning to I commented half under my breath, "Not just anyone can take her place." Adriana María calmly turned her back on me and continued watching television. Then something very strange happened. My grudge disappeared and I was again invaded by a sense of well-being. One can't even understand oneself. I knew that that woman wasn't the missus, but while I couldn't see her face, I let myself be deceived by appearances. Probably you can get out of all this rather bitter consequences as to what Diana meant to me. Is she just her hair, or even less, the wave of her hair on her shoulders, and the shape of her body and the way she sits? I would like to believe that this isn't so, but it's hard putting confused thoughts into words.

You might say that Diana's right, that watchmaking is second nature to me, that I tend to look closely at minor details. I believe, however, that the previous scene, insig-

nificant if remembered by itself, placed next to the other
events I'm telling you about, takes on meaning and helps
make them understandable.

XVII

For a whole long hour I again took refuge in my work.
When I came back to the house, Adriana María was
showing Ceferina the Irala family tree. It had been
prepared, for a steep price, by the same crook at the Cattle Fair, who told them that they were descended from an
Irala from colonial times. As Aldini says, only I would
have the luck to get a family so completely different from
what you see nowadays. I looked over my sister-in-law's
shoulder and when I made out Diana's name on one of
the last branches—I'm there next to her, joined by a
dash—I was moved. Poor thing, she's in luck with a jerk
like me. Suddenly I looked up and saw that Ceferina was
laughing. Probably she was laughing at my sister-in-law's
vanity, though maybe she caught me passing my hand
over my eyes. When she wants to catch other people's
absurdities the old woman is like a hawk.
One thing seemed obvious: in my troubles I would do
well not to ask for understanding from the women around
me. Ceferina took on a smug air as if to say, "Didn't I tell
you so?" I would like to know what the old woman was
blaming me for. I didn't marry my sister-in-law, I married the missus. You'll say, "It's a well-known fact, a man
thinks he's marrying a woman and he's marrying a whole
family." Let me make it clear that, if necessary, I'd marry
Diana all over again, even if I had to carry Adriana
María, Don Martín, and Martincito on piggyback. It's
true that in those days I was really sorry that my sister-in-

law looked so much like the missus. I was always confusing one with the other, which kept startling me by making me feel that I had Diana back. I'd say to myself, I'm going to do my best to make sure she doesn't fool me again. Believe me, in my situation, it's not good to have a similar person in the house, because it always reminds you of the real one's absence.

Maybe I already told you that I'm a little finicky; for example, I can't stand the smell of food in people's clothing or in their hair. Diana is always pulling my leg; she says that maybe I'm not interested in ancestors but I have the standards of a snob. Who knows what Ceferina was cooking that afternoon; the truth is it was as if you were having a Turkish bath in garlic vapors. I must have complained, because Adriana María asked me:

"Does that nice smell bother you? It makes me hungry! If you want, come into my room."

Before going I looked back. Ceferina was winking her eye at me, although she knows perfectly well that I don't like people to start thinking nonsense. My vexation must have been apparent on my face, because Adriana María asked me worriedly:

"What's the matter with you, you poor thing?" She leaned her hands on my shoulders, stared at me, and without hesitating kicked the door shut and persisted in a very affectionate tone, "What's the matter?"

I wanted to free myself from her arms and leave the room, because I didn't know what to say to her. I couldn't mention Ceferina's wink without reviving the resentment between the two women and maybe without suggesting that I disapproved of her lack of tact in the very innocent act of closing the door. So, therefore, I didn't give the right reason, but rather the usual one. I did so, intending to assure my sister-in-law's sympathy.

"I wonder if it isn't just too outrageous," I murmured.

I must have been pale, because she started to rub me as if she were trying to stimulate the circulation of my blood all over my body:

"What's so outrageous?" she exclaimed very gaily.

"Do you think it was necessary?"

"That what was necessary?"

She pronounced each word separately. She seemed like an idiot.

"Locking her up in the mental institute," I explained.

I don't understand women. Without apparent cause, Adriana María passed from excitement to fatigue. A doctor who was seeing the missus told me that this happens when the blood pressure suddenly goes down. Now my sister-in-law seemed exhausted, bored, without the energy to talk or even to live. I was about to advise her to watch her blood pressure when she murmured, after visible effort, "It's for her own good."

"I'm not sure," I answered. "Who knows what suffering the poor thing's going through, while we're doing what we feel like doing."

She laughed in a strange way and asked, "What we feel like doing?"

"Putting someone away, I mean, you can have it."

"It'll be over soon."

"We shouldn't fool ourselves," I insisted. "The poor thing's in an insane asylum."

In a tone that I didn't like, she replied, "Enough with the poor thing. Others don't have the luck of having someone to pay for a luxurious insane asylum."

"An asylum is an asylum," I complained.

She answered me, "Luxury is luxury."

I had hoped to get along with her, that she'd be a true sister in my desolation, but you see the atrocious things she said to me. And she had in reserve an even further surprise. When a cuckoo clock began to strike eight, she squirmed as if something were driving her crazy and she screamed piercingly, "Don't bother me with that woman again."

Did you hear that: she called her own sister that woman.

Without saying a word I left the room. Adriana María must have been furious, because she raised her voice and very clearly mumbled, "Rotten bitch," "How long will it go on?" "What does he see in her." I didn't pay any attention and walked away.

I bumped into Ceferina in the hallway. She immediately asked me, "So you didn't give her her way?"

In a fit of rage I answered, "I'm not eating home tonight."

XVIII

Not to make things worse than they are, but, believe me, in a situation like mine, without a friend to listen to me and advise me, solitude becomes frankly unrewarding. Tell me, to whom could I unburden myself? For inexplicable reasons, my sister-in-law had taken a dislike to Diana. Ceferina, why fool myself, never loved her. The kid was a kid. My father-in-law — the poor thing was no less upset that I — blamed me for putting her away and hated me. I remember that I pondered, If only I had a dog, like lame Aldini, then I could chat about my troubles and comfort myself. Maybe if I had paid attention to Diana, when she cried out for one, I would have avoided misfortunes.

As soon as I went out that night, I regretted my fit of rage and wondered what I would do with myself. It's a good thing that in the midst of so many misfortunes I hadn't completely lost my appetite, because leaning on a table in any old bar you can have a more entertaining time than going around in circles on the street.

Perhaps because I had thought of Aldini, I found him at The Bend. I couldn't see any other explanation. At some point Diana had made me observe that this is quite common.

"You here?" I asked.

Aldini was alone, facing a glass of wine.

"The missus is sick," he answered.

"Mine too."

"And they say there's no such thing as coincidences. If I hang around, Elvira is unreasonable and insists on making me dinner. I lied to her so that she wouldn't tire herself out."

"You don't say."

"I made up the story that my friends had invited me out to dinner. I don't like to lie to her."

I told him, "I'll invite you, that way you haven't lied to her."

"We'll have dinner together. You don't have to invite me."

I tried to explain that if I didn't invite him he would be lying to the missus, but I got entangled in the explanation. We ordered stew.

"I never thought I'd find you at The Bend," I assured him sincerely.

"And they say there's no such thing as coincidences," he answered.

"Coincidences?" I asked. "What do coincidences have to do with it?"

"Both of us at The Bend. Both of us have sick wives."

"You're right," I admitted.

He's intelligent, that Aldini. He repeated several times, "Both of us have sick wives."

"One gets kind of disoriented," I remarked.

As the stew took a while, I emptied the bread basket. At the back of my neck someone spoke.

"Don't pay any attention to this big hypocrite," I turned around; it was Fats Picardo, who pointed at me with his finger and said, "He smuggled his sister-in-law into the house, and she's the spitting image of the missus."

He winked his eye (like Ceferina, a while ago), he didn't wait for us to invite him, he took a seat, asked for a serving of stew and with the airs of a grand personage took his two or three puffs on the half-crushed cigarette Aldini had left in the ashtray.

From the billiard tables a blond, big-headed gentleman, shorter than normal height, stocky in his fitted suit, came toward us. It looked to me like his hair was combed with pomade and he seemed very clean and even shiny. From a long way off you could tell that he was the kind who gets manicured in the big barbershops downtown. Fats Picardo hurriedly introduced him.

"This is the doctor."

"Dr. Jorge Rivaroli," the fellow clarified. "If it's not an inconvenience, I'll join you."

Picardo pulled up a chair for him. As if we had nothing to talk about, there was a long silence. I continued eating bread.

"The weather is rather changeable lately," the doctor remarked.

"The humidity is the worst part," Aldini replied.

Picardo said to me, "You promised me that you might get interested in the numbers, maybe."

"I don't play," I answered.

"Well done," the doctor approved. "There's too much insecurity in this world for us to add yet another game of chance."

Picardo looked at me anxiously.

"You promised," he insisted.

The doctor talked him out of it. "One mustn't bore people, Picardito."

"What's to drink, gentlemen?" the owner, Don Pepino in person, came over to our table as soon as he saw Rivaroli.

"Wine for everybody," the doctor ordered. "Red, of course."

I prefer white wine, but I didn't say a thing.

"Half a bottle of soda water," Aldini added.

Though totally unhappy, Picardo couldn't keep from being mischievous.

"The gentleman's missus is sick," he explained, pointing to me, "but he doesn't complain, because he brought the sister-in-law, who's identical, into the house."

"It's not the same thing," I protested.

They all laughed. With my answer I paved the way for them to discuss my private affairs, which displeased me profoundly.

Picardo commented, "I'll bet that in the dark you confuse her with the missus."

Not in vain do they say that out of the mouths of fools comes the truth.

"I find," Aldini pensively remarked, and I was grateful to him for drawing the attention toward himself, "that in the evening light a rather strange thing happens. If I tell you you're going to laugh."

Out of loyalty I advised him, "Don't tell us."

"Why shouldn't he tell us?" the doctor asked, and served a round of house wine. "It seems to me we're among friends."

Aldini admitted, "Maybe because my eyesight is clouding over, but when there's little light, the missus looks prettier to me, how shall I say, as if she were young. It's very strange: in those moments I think that's how I see her, the girl she was when she was young, and I love her more."

"And if you put your glasses on?" Picardo asked.

"What can I tell you, I see details which, the less said, the better."

"I don't recognize you," I said. "Generally you're not so indiscreet."

"Well, you know," he protested, "once in a great while I can get a little tipsy."

His voice thickening, the doctor pointed out, "The gentleman is a lover of beauty."

Picardo pointed to me with his finger.

"That one too. If you don't believe me, Doctor, ask about his missus and his sister-in-law. They're hot stuff."

"Don't be a pest, Picardito," the doctor scolded him.

"I'm not pestering him," Picardo protested. "I'll bet you don't know, Doctor, what happened to the poor guy. In connivance with a German dog trainer he put the missus in the nuthouse and now he regrets it."

The doctor advised me sincerely, "Take it in your stride. You know, besides, that Picardito is not malicious."

"Look," I answered him, "I'm not paying any attention, because I know Picardo; but there's no doubt that he's malicious."

"His meanness comes from the bottom of his heart," the waiter supported me, as he served another round of stew.

Picardo persisted. "Now he walks around like a ghost, because he regrets he did it and he wants to take her out of the nuthouse."

How did he find out? My eternal sermon: in the alley all news somehow gets around.

"Pardon me if I'm meddling," Rivaroli said. "May I ask you something?"

Frankly I didn't want the fellow to get mixed up in my affairs. But because I couldn't find a way of saying no, I said yes.

"There's no one better than the doctor to give you a hand, if you really want to get the missus out," Picardo remarked.

I must have been quite nervous, because the amount of

stew and bread that I ate that night was outrageous, not to mention that I overdid it with the wine.

"Reasons of professional ethics induce me to submit you to a question," the doctor explained. "Do you remember if you filled out the pertinent authorization?"

"Pertinent?"

"To have your spouse admitted."

"I didn't sign anything," I answered.

"You did well," he said to me. "Never sign anything. Do you know if the missus gave her authorization in writing?"

"No, that I don't know."

"If she didn't, we have something to stand on and we can act."

They brought me the bill.

"I'm paying," the doctor said.

"No, I'm paying," I replied, "Aldini's and mine."

Picardo enthusiastically commented, "Now you'll see how the doctor makes them dance on the tightrope." He didn't say who.

"I am entirely at your service," the doctor assured me as we left. "When the moment is right, send Picardito over to me. I promise you I'll be cheaper than the hospital, with the added advantage that you'll have the missus back home."

As it had begun to drizzle, the doctor offered to take us in his car. Aldini and I insisted that he not go out of his way, because after so much socializing, it's a real rest to be alone with a friend. We went on our way to the alley. The drizzle turned into a downpour, Aldini's limp slowed our pace, our clothes got soaked, and I started to wonder if it wouldn't have been better to accept Rivaroli's invitation. Under a cornice we waited for the shower to pass. Aldini suddenly said to me:

"Don't get involved with lawyers. They'll take the shirt off your back."

"One must be fair," I answered. "Picardo's right about

one thing. If I want to get Diana back, I shouldn't create difficulties."

"I wonder if tonight's conversation hasn't committed you. It's a good question."

"I didn't say yes."

"You didn't say no. It's better not to have a creature like that for an enemy. Or the nuthouse guys either."

"Well, ol' man, one has to choose. If I want to get her out, I have to step on someone's toes."

"Do you think the missus could have given the German an authorization?"

"Why would she give it to him?"

"I don't know. I'm asking."

"You're asking for some reason."

The rain stopped a bit, so we continued on our way, Aldini determined to walk slowly, me pulling him by the arm, which was incredibly tiring. When we crossed the street, the old boy refused to jump over the water, or couldn't, and he got wet up to his ankles. He remarked thoughtfully:

"If afterward it turns out that she signed it, who knows what complications the lawyer will get you into."

"You think so?"

"Slander or something or other." After a pause, he added, "I wouldn't like to have the nuthouse guys for enemies."

We had reached the alley. Aldini's reflections had bored me.

"Well, I'm going to have to step on someone's toes," I commented. "I'm going to hit the hay, I'm falling off my feel I'm so tired."

"Lucky you. I still have to take Naughty Boy for a walk, besides the tea I'll have to make for Elvira."

All the lights were out at home. Because of the stew I spent the whole night dreaming nightmares and other nonsense.

56

XIX

If I tell you that the next morning Ceferina treated me with remarkable consideration, maybe you won't believe me. However, it's the plain truth. Not for nothing does Don Martín repeat that a woman's mood is as changeable as the weather in Buenos Aires.

We were having *maté* when I said to Ceferina, "If any customer comes, tell them I won't be in the shop till the afternoon."

Ceferina commented to my sister-in-law, "You heard him, now he spends his mornings out."

She acted as if I weren't there, but don't think that she was being contemptuous. From a mile away you could detect in her voice a tone of admiration and puzzlement. I could have sworn, besides, that the two women weren't as hostile to each other as usual. Who can understand them?

"Where are you going?" Adriana María asked.

"I'll be back for lunch," I answered.

They looked at each other. I almost felt sorry for them.

As the weather had changed, I walked along in high spirits, so that I reached the neighborhood of the mental institute quite soon. I'll admit that I leaned against the gate of the Clinic for Small Animals because in sight of the institute my courage began to falter. I wasn't afraid for myself. I didn't trust my ability to argue and to convince and I wondered if my visit would make Diana's situation worse; if the poor thing wouldn't pay later for my clumsiness and bad temper.

Of course, by fearing for Diana, I was fearing for myself, because I can't live without her. I think Diana herself once told me that all love, and especially mine, is selfish. On the other hand, if I didn't speak to

Samaniego, I'd risk a scolding from Diana the next day. "You didn't stick your neck out for me."

I perked up my spirits as well as I could, crossed Baigorria and rang the doorbell of the institute. An orderly took me into Dr. Reger Samaniego's office, where, after waiting awhile, I was personally received by his assistant, Dr. Campolongo. This was a fellow with a very pale and round shaven face, and so well combed that you'd think he used a compass and a ruler to distribute his hairs.

First detail I didn't like: as soon as he had me there, he locked the door. There was another door to the inside.

I could give you an inventory of that office, which I won't forget as long as I live. To the right I saw one of those standing clocks made by T. Derême that, if you'll spare them the attention every machine deserves, are, in general, punctual. The institute one had been stopped at 1:13 since God knows when. On the left there was a metal file cabinet and a sink with a shelf, where I glimpsed several syringes. In the middle was the desk with a prescription pad, some books, a telephone, a bell in the shape of a turtle with a brass shell. The desk was black wood, intricately wrought with a trimming of little heads with expressions and all, fine craftsmanship, but it repelled me a bit, because it seemed like it would bring bad luck. There were also armchairs, with very dark *repoussé* leather backs and seats, decorated with the same little heads that bring bad luck. On the back wall, among diplomas, there was a picture of characters dressed in tunics and helmets.

Campolongo said to me, "You're going to have to forgive Dr. Reger Samaniego. He cannot attend to you now. He's on the fifth."

"On the fifth?"

"Yes, on the fifth floor. In surgery."

"I didn't know," I answered him, to hide my disappointment, "that you did operations here."

"Surgery," he explained to me, arrogantly, "at the present time enriches the arsenal of advanced psychiatric therapy. In what can I be of assistance to you, Mr. Bordenave?"

"I came for news of the missus."

Campolongo opened a drawer and started going through files, which took him a time that seemed endless to me. Finally he said, "The news, generally speaking, is good. I would say that your missus is responding favorably to treatment."

In order not to rush into anything, because the next step was decisive, I asked him a question to gain time.

"What's that picture about?"

"A Roman motif. Dr. Reger Samaniego will explain it to you. I think it's a king with his wife."

Arming myself with courage, I took advantage of the coincidence and asked, "Do you think, Doctor, that I could see mine?"

Leisurely, Campolongo put the files away, closed the drawer and said to me, "In this particular case, the visit of any person close to the patient is not very advisable. Of course, I am not excluding the possibility that Dr. Reger Samaniego will be of a different opinion and accede, dear Mr. Bordenave, to your friendly request."

"If you don't mind, I'll wait for the doctor."

"I'm very much afraid that you won't be able to see him."

In short, with his friendly air, he had said no first and immediately, to fool me, said maybe, and finally, no. When you've gotten your hopes up to see a person you miss, and then they say you can't see her, your grief can be very great. Sort of regaining my self-control, I asked him, "Are you able to give me the approximate date when the missus will come back home?"

Campolongo assured me, "As to that, I can't answer you, since it will all depend, as you can well understand, on how much the patient responds to treatment."

"Must I resign myself," I asked him, "to returning home empty-handed?"

With an air of extreme courtesy, Campolongo smiled and leaned forward.

"Correct," he said.

Maybe he thought I completely accepted it.

"It so happens," I warned him, "that I'm not going to resign myself."

He looked at me, surprised.

"You will have to speak to Dr. Reger Samaniego."

"When?" I asked.

"When the doctor receives you."

Meanwhile, the missus remains locked up and I can't see her."

"Don't get nervous."

"How do you expect me not to get nervous? I didn't think the missus was in prison."

"She's ill."

"I didn't know a sanatorium was a jail."

"Don't get nervous."

"If I get nervous, will you put me away?"

I thought, At least I'll be closer to Diana.

Campolongo got up from the chair, went around the desk gently, as if I were sleeping and he didn't want to wake me up, and went over to the sink. Meanwhile he repeated in a mechanical way, "Don't get nervous."

He spoke like someone trying to calm down and amuse a sick child or a dog.

"If I get nervous, will you give me an injection? A tranquilizer? God help you. I'll have the place closed."

Campolongo stopped to look at me. I think that my words angered him, by the way he said, "Don't make threats."

"And who do you think you are? Who are you to tell me what I should or shouldn't do? I'll have you know that my lawyer is perfectly informed of this visit. If I don't call at noon, he will act."

"A lawyer? Who is he?"

"You'll find out when the time comes."

"Don't get so excited."

"How would you like me to get?"

"I suggest that you make an appointment, for today or tomorrow, with Dr. Reger Samaniego. Maybe he will let you see the patient."

Because I wasn't expecting anything, I took these conciliatory words as unconditional surrender. To be sure, I asked, "Are you being sincere?"

"Why shouldn't I be sincere?"

"Do you think Samaniego will give me permission?"

The question seemed quite obsequious to me. Campolongo recovered his superior tone.

"My good man," he said, "we shall see about that. I told you my honest professional opinion. If Dr. Reger Samaniego decides something else, I won't be the one to oppose him. The doctor knows what he's doing!"

"As far as I'm concerned, I'd advise you to fix your clock." I pointed to the T. Derême. "A clock that doesn't work gives a bad impression. People think: Here everything works the same."

What do I gain by saying impolite things that people don't understand? Campolongo listened to me expressionlessly, perhaps furious, but he had already gotten his way in denying me Diana and, on top of that, in calling me his good man. On my way home, my spirits were down to the ground.

XX

When I arrived, Adriana María was busy cleaning up, Martincito was not yet back from school or Ceferina from shopping. I went into my room, wrapped myself in the

61

black and blue poncho Ceferina had given me as a wedding present, and lay down on the bed. The temperature had frankly gone down or perhaps my vexation at the mental hospital had given me a chill.

A while later, without knocking on the door, Adriana María came in. She caught me by surprise, because now she was in house clothes, but really in her underwear which, on a morning like that, was hard to understand.

"Aren't you going to catch cold?" I asked her.

"The house is warm and, what can I tell you, I still have young blood."

"What do you mean, it's warm?" I answered. "Going around exposing yourself to drafts doesn't make any sense."

Adriana María snorted, dropped into a chair between the bed and the window, and looked at me with curiosity on her face.

"What's wrong?" she asked.

"Nothing," I said.

"Are you ill?"

"What makes you think that? I'm perfectly fine."

"Did you tire yourself out?"

"A little. But if you want to know, you're the one who looks down in the mouth. Is anything wrong?"

"I'm worried because the kid's not back from school yet," she said. She smiled and asked me in a different tone, "Am I a bore? Am I bothering you?"

"Of course not."

I looked at her so that she'd believe me and I met with the very picture of suffocation: messy, sprawled out on the chair with her legs open and her breasts half-exposed, she was so strange that her voice, perfectly normal, surprised me when she asked, "What you least want now is a woman, right?"

"Why do you say that?"

"Well I don't blame you. You know something? I'm a real tiger, too."

I felt lousy, I was very sad, I was thinking about the missus, whom I wouldn't see till God knows when and this woman, looking like that, was talking nonsense which didn't have the slightest connection.

I assured her, "I'm not a tiger."

It was useless to protest. Adriana María asked me, "Isn't what you have at home better?"

I was going to tell her that frankly I didn't understand, when I opened my eyes out of curiosity or fear. The show was not comforting. Breathing heavily, and moving from side to side, my sister-in-law brought to mind Wild Gaucho Asadurian, in the Luna Park Boxing Ring, seconds before launching an attack. When she turned her head around, as if she couldn't breathe, she must have seen something through the window, because she quickly stood up. I crouched instinctively, but Adriana María was already out of the room and shouting to me in a whisper, "Martincito! Martincito!"

You'll laugh if I tell you that in the silence of the room I heard the beating of my heart. I finally went to check my Escasany watch. The kid had returned from school with commendable punctuality. All that to-do about worrying because he hadn't come was, therefore, unjustifiable.

I didn't have time to settle my thoughts, because, just to annoy me, another visitor came into the room. It was the kid. Like his mother, he didn't ask permission before entering. All the Iralas are alike, but Diana is the queen of the family.

The kid planted himself in the middle of the room, standing with his arms crossed, tensely, frantically, extraordinarily still. Standing like that, in his school apron, which was long on him because his mother calculated a sudden growth which hadn't occurred, he reminded me of God knows what engraving of a general in exile, looking at the sea. Martincito stared at me severely, almost menacingly, and from above, which took him some effort because if I'm not mistaken, with him standing and me in the bed, we're the same height. As if he couldn't control himself, he took a little step from time to time and reeled in his hurry to regain his stiff position. I think he produced a kind of buzz. I started to get tired of having to put up with him, so I said, "Hey, you look like a statue."

He really looked like an angry little monkey when he came over to the bed, as if he wanted to attack me, and with a quick grab he pulled off my poncho, which flapped in the air like a big blue bird and, on falling, surrounded me in darkness. You can't imagine how I struggled to disentangle myself. When I finally stuck my head out, I found Martincito completely changed, not at all menacing, but rather, stoop-shouldered. He opened his mouth and looked at me in confusion.

"I've had it with your pantomime," I said to him.

I jumped out of bed, took him by the arm and put him outside. As soon as I let go, he turned around to look at me with his mouth open.

Just in case, I looked at myself too, because I remembered nightmares in which you think you're dressed and suddenly you find yourself naked. I was awake; my suit was wrinkled but decent.

XXI

As I was hungry, I went to the kitchen to get a piece of bread. I went outside to be alone, but I found lame Aldini stationed with the dog. Don't think I was displeased; it's the women I'm tired of. The sun was comforting.

"Give me a piece of bread," Aldini said.

We chewed in perfect silence. After a while I couldn't

keep it in any longer and I gave a detailed account of my conversation with Dr. Campolongo.

"The doctor told me that my visit could harm Diana. Can you believe that nonsense?"

"I've heard that visits from relatives are harmful to these patients."

"Yeah, but I'm not just a relative," I answered with legitimate self-righteousness.

"If I were you I wouldn't give Rivaroli a chance to get his foot in the door."

"And Reger, should I call him up?"

"More bread," Aldini said, and stuck out his hand. He ate thoughtfully.

I persisted. "Should I call him?"

"No," he said. "I would be patient."

"Very easy, to be patient. It's not Elvira who's locked up."

"You're right," he agreed, "but it won't do you any good to call Reger."

"Why?"

"Because if you call him, you put your cards on the table and maybe you'll have to do something."

"What?"

"That's what we don't know. That's why it's better not to call him."

"I feel like calling him."

"If you can't get him to see you or if he gives you a flat no, you'll find yourself in the sad need of resorting to the lawyer so that the doctors won't walk all over you."

"Do you think that I'm protecting Diana if I don't do anything?"

"Of course. If you don't call, they don't know what you're up to and they'll hurry and return her to protect themselves."

Aldini always excelled in intelligence.

Shouting at the top of their lungs, the women were telling me that lunch was getting cold.

XXII

In the afternoon I took refuge in the shop, where I had more than enough work, because in those days they brought me a whole bunch of clocks. With the money earned I could have afforded Diana the life of luxury she never tired of asking for, but the miserable money came in when the missus couldn't take advantage of it.

The same old thing: it was enough for me to put the water on to boil for *maté* for there to be a knock at the door. An older gentleman appeared, escorted by two workers who were carrying, on a kind of stretcher made of sticks, the clock from the Lorenzutti factory. The man explained to me that he was the foreman, that the clock hadn't been working for years, and that now he wanted it, in perfect working order, for a party they were giving on Sunday. I told him to take it to another watchmaker, that frankly I had more than enough work (which, once said, seemed to me the kind of arrogance that can bring bad luck). The foreman didn't give in an inch and asked me in a way that seemed offensive, "How much are you asking, to have the clock by Saturday?"

"I wouldn't take it for a hundred dollars," I told him, to make it clear that I was flatly rejecting it.

"It's a deal," he answered.

Before I could protest, he had left with the workers.

I had no choice but to move the work I had on the repair table to the side table, and to take apart the factory clock. With bitter presentiments I wondered if all the money that persisted in coming in so abundantly wouldn't finally be useless. Prolonged anxiety tends to afflict man with superstitions and schemes.

I had already put the water on to boil, when there was another knock at the door. I remember that I wondered if this time they weren't bringing the Big Ben. It was Martincito, who came in with a book.

"A present from Grandpa, because I got good grades. I want you to read it."

"I have to take this clock apart."

"Some little clock!"

"It's the original Big Ben."

Martincito looked at it, dazzled, while he absent-mindedly moved his hands above the clocks on the other table. I thought it wouldn't be long before he touched them.

"Be careful with the customers' clocks," I warned him.

If I give him what he deserves, even though it's his fault, Diana—when she comes back—will never forgive me because she loves him as if he were her own son. Would Diana come back? If I wasn't paying attention, I took her return for granted, but if I started thinking, I wasn't sure.

"I don't think it's a book for boys. Grandpa, who's a big cheapskate, maybe already gave it to Mama and to Aunt Diana when they were little."

"Why do you say it's not a book for boys?"

"There's a prince who's changed into a beast. If he gets a girl to love him, he becomes a prince again."

"You don't say," I said.

He told me that if I didn't believe him I should read it. I promised I would. He persisted.

"Start now."

I had to obey. I admit that the book interested me quite a bit, because the beast finally gets a young lady to love him and becomes a prince again.

"I like it."

"Why do you lie?" he asked.

"I'm not lying. I swear, I too was a beast until I met your aunt Diana."

He was annoying me, because he was again moving his

fingers above the clocks. I knew he was thinking about something else, but when I found out what it was, I was surprised. He said, "Mama is bad. She doesn't love Aunt Diana. I love her."

Half the Lorenzutti clock almost fell out of my hands.

"You love Diana?" I asked him.

"More than anybody. Who wouldn't love her?"

"I love her, too."

"I know. That's why you and I must be friends."

Martincito was right. At that moment I would have offered him the druggist's Roskopf watch to play with.

"We must be friends," I said.

He looked all around and asked me, "Would you dare to sign a blood pact?"

"Of course I would."

"I have to tell you something."

"Tell me."

"You're not going to tell anybody in the whole world what I tell you?"

"Nobody in the whole world."

"Not even Mama?"

"Not even her."

"Don't pay any attention to Mama, because she's always trying to separate you from Aunt Diana."

"Nobody will separate me from your aunt Diana."

"You're not going to pay attention to Mama? Swear it."

I swore.

XXIII

At night Adriana María went past my door several times in her underwear. Suddenly I couldn't control myself. I got up and called her, with a finger over my lips

68

to indicate that she shouldn't make a sound. She came quickly. Looking at her so close up I could imagine that she was the missus. I said to her, "Can I ask you something?"

She said yes. When I was about to speak, she put a finger on her lips to indicate that I shouldn't make a sound, she took me by the arm, led me to the middle of the room, went on tiptoe to close the door, came back and looked at me in a way that, sincerely, made me feel sure that we understood each other.

"The old lady," she explained, "has a sharp ear. Say what you want. Go ahead."

I got up the courage and said, "Do you think that I'll do Diana any harm if I visit her?"

"Who?"

"Diana. That's what a doctor in the mental hospital said."

She spoke in a casual little voice.

"So you went to the mental hospital this morning?" Before I could open my mouth, she was shouting at me without bothering at all if Ceferina could hear her. "What do I care if you do her any harm or good? I always thought you were more of a man, but I swear, now I understand my sister and I even sympathize with her and I congratulate her with all my heart for going after the dog trainer."

"What are you saying?" I asked her. "You're going to explain yourself right this minute."

She answered, "You're stubborn, but you're no man."

Her fury at moments made her look like she had an upset stomach, or even indecent, which distressed me, because she looked so much like Diana. She said that she wouldn't say another thing to me so that I wouldn't spend the night crying in the old lady's lap.

Of course I spent the night brooding, tossing and turning in bed. Suddenly I shouted, "What can that fit of anger matter to me, if Diana's locked up in the mental hospital?" I hadn't finished the sentence when I was startled by a doubt. Or isn't she locked up? What was Adriana Maria suggesting? This new suspicion perhaps clarified my morning's conversation with Dr. Campolongo. He was against my seeing her, I said to myself, for the simple reason that Diana wasn't in the clinic. To get rid of me for good he invented that nonsense that my visits would do her harm.

A man thinks in a strange way at night. He considers believable everything that is threatening or frightening, but easily puts aside thoughts that could calm him down. So for hours, I found it natural that the doctors would say that they had admitted her, though Diana might not have set foot in the institute. Why would they? To cover up for a dog trainer? The Hippocratic oath requires another kind of ethics.

I'm so crazy and wretched that when I reached the conclusion Diana was in the institute for a moment I was actually glad.

When I was finally falling asleep, I heard footsteps on the gravel path. I lay still to hear better. As the guy outside didn't move either, there was perfect silence. The one who gets tired first is going to move, I thought. The guy outside must have gotten tired because I heard the footsteps again. I ran to the bureau, opened a drawer and in my hurry couldn't find the Eibar. It's a revolver with a mother-of-pearl handle that my late father left me. On the other hand, I found the flashlight. I ran to the window, opened it, and barely had time to shine it on a man who scrambled over the fence and disappeared. I could have sworn it was the helper from the dog school, but I said to myself that a working man doesn't become a thief at night.

XXIV

The next morning, while I got up and dressed, I continued to brood, so that without thinking what I was doing—without combing my hair even, or shaving—I went into the kitchen to have some *maté*. As soon as she saw me, Ceferina came to meet me and, looking into my eyes, asked me, "What's the matter?"

Drinking her *maté* in the rocking chair, my sister-in-law hid her laughter, as if she thought it was very funny. I shouldn't say this, but sometimes I compare her to a large-sized vixen licking her chops beforehand over the naughty things she's going to do. Her eyes shine, she has an ample figure, like Diana, and the same rosy skin. Almost the only difference, you already know, is the color of her hair. I remember that I thought, It's incredible that she's so bad and she looks so much like the missus.

"You've got rings under your eyes," Ceferina said. "You look pale."

"Greenish," Adriana María corrected.

"Are you feeling ill?"

Adriana María said, "He probably spent the night sighing over his little wife. If he only knew what Diana was up to. But don't talk to him about another woman."

I couldn't believe my ears. I swear that on occasions I'm surprised by the liberties women take. I would like to know what they talk about when they're among themselves. Even though they don't get along, they form a kind of trade union.

"Don't laugh," the old lady said to her.

"Do you think I have any desire left to laugh?"

"My, how you shouted at him last night."

I protested on the spot, "She didn't shout at me."

"Do you think I'm deaf?" Ceferina commented, and she passed me the *maté*.

"Last night there was a guy in the garden."

"I heard footsteps, too," the old lady said. "You have to fix the kitchen window."

"What's the matter with the window?" Adriana María said.

"It doesn't lock. One night we're going to find a guy inside."

"Let's hope so," Adriana María said.

I asked, "Has Martincito already left?"

"If he hadn't, he'd be late," the old lady explained.

"He's not going to wait for you to wake up," said Adriana María.

I find that it never fails. On nights when I don't sleep a wink, I end up oversleeping.

Adriana María announced, "I'm going out."

"Where are you going?" the old lady asked.

"I have my things to do too. Or is only the man here allowed to go out without explanations?"

It seemed that she was talking to me. What do I care if she goes or doesn't go out?

When she left us alone, the old lady leaned her hands on my shoulders and asked me, "What's the matter, Lucho?"

"Nothing," I said to her.

"You don't even trust me?"

Look how affectionate she is when she wants to be.

"If that's the way you feel, I'll tell you. I don't know what's the matter with me, but I wonder if Diana will ever come back."

"You're just like Picardo. When that raggedy Mari left him, he'd spend the day in The Bend and from the back he'd shout at the owner, 'Pepino, you think she'll come back?'"

I said to her, "Very funny." She asked me why Diana wouldn't come back.

"People keep insinuating it."

"Don't listen to your sister-in-law."

"There's another reason. Maybe I'm just being crazy. I'm earning so much money that it makes me think. The quantity is what amazes me. I wonder if the money is coming in on purpose because I'm not going to have anything to spend it on."

"If that's why, don't worry," she said. "If they leave Diana in the insane asylum forever, what you earn will not be enough to maintain her."

Perhaps she was right, but that fact didn't matter; she didn't understand and I didn't know how to explain it.

"Yesterday they came in with such a big clock that it seems to me it must bring bad luck. They're paying me an outrageous sum. Nobody can get it out of my head that there's something bad about all this. You're going to laugh: as if I were afraid of catching something, I've been working on the clock hurriedly and anxiously."

"Anxious about what?"

"That Diana won't come back."

For a little while she looked at me as if she were perplexed; then she asked me very gently, "Do you know why there's no hope for this world?"

I assured her that I didn't.

She said, "Because one man's dream is another's nightmare."

"I don't understand," I admitted.

"Without going any further, think of politics."

"What does politics have to do with it?"

I tried to explain the difference between politics and my fondness for Diana. She interrupted me:

"Without going any further, think of elections and revolutions. Half the population is satisfied and the other half desperate."

"That's news," I said.

For some time past she's been getting easily annoyed.

"That's news, that's news," she repeated with that

damn arrogance that comes from being so intelligent. "Under the same roof you're praying for Diana to come back, and Adriana María, for her not to come back."

"You think so?" I asked her.

"How couldn't I think so? And if you push me a little, I'll tell you that I wouldn't complain if Diana stayed in there and rotted to death."

A good thing, I thought, that Martincito's still my friend.

XXV

I spent the rest of the morning with the factory's Ausonia clock. I worked in a great hurry to finish, as if I were convinced that while I was busy with that big clumsy thing, anything could be happening to the missus in the mental institute. At eleven-thirty, quite relieved, I put the machine back in its case. Of course I would keep the clock under observation for at least twenty-four hours before returning it.

Aldini has explained to me so many times that I shouldn't allow superstition to overwhelm me, because it saddens the spirit.

In search of some concrete information about lunch, I went to the kitchen to see the women. I remember that I said to myself, as if I were talking to my sister-in-law, You're back soon, and that I couldn't help wondering where she had gone. Their backs to the door, they were busy with the stove and pots, and from time to time they put their heads together to tell secrets. The fact that they were such good friends now left me indifferent, because it was enough to think things over for a second to understand that the only reason for all that friendship was their resentment toward Diana. They told secrets out of habit but they couldn't hide their hatred.

I felt like chatting with Martincito (perhaps I was feeling quite lonely) but I finally decided to head for The Bend, because I didn't have the energy to put up with the women's faces and innuendos all during lunch. I passed by my room to tidy myself up a bit, picked up my jacket, and from the kitchen door I shouted:

"I'm having lunch out."

As soon as I was in the alley, Picardo descended on me. Right to Aldini's he talked nonstop, to convince me that his greatest desire was for me to place a big, whole-hearted bet on a mare that was going to be the hit of the century at Palermo on Saturday. While I said, "I don't bet, I didn't bring any money," he insisted, "You can't let me down," and dwelled at length on details, pronouncing the mare's name, which was foreign, with some tongue (and even false teeth) difficulties.

"I don't bet," I repeated.

"Buy eighty tickets."

"I didn't bring any money."

"I'll give you credit. If the doctor finds out, I'll lose my job, because he's a fanatic about hard cash. You're not going to let down a childhood friend, are you? I'm asking you just in case the mare comes out a loser. But rest assured, you're going to win a lot of dough."

I told him positively that I didn't bet, but who can make a weak guy like Picardo accept no for an answer? He repeated to infinity, "a lot of dough," and stated, "You'll pay the cost over the winnings. The doctor and I want to give you satisfaction."

I said to him, "I'm not going to pay you anything."

He promised me that he was going to buy the tickets. I went into Aldini's and without difficulty recruited him for lunch at The Bend. Doña Elvira, who was a little better, commented, "I would like to believe that you two

75

aren't up to something. As soon as I'm better, I'm going to take a walk over to The Bend to see if Pepino hasn't employed a platoon of barmaids."

She was joking, I assure you.

During lunch Aldini was not at his best. He and the missus are religiously following the television soap opera, "The Secret Shadows," about some doctors, dressed in frock coats and top hats, who, in order to do transplants, or autopsies and vivisections, steal corpses from the local cemetery. A scary story about the dawn of science which, if I'm not mistaken, takes place in Edinburgh in the days of the Queen of England, in which the actors put white plaster over their faces and play the role of the living dead. Although I made him see that he was ruining my appetite with his details, I couldn't make him change the subject.

Afterward I went back home with the best intention of working at the shop. Since I hadn't slept all last night, I couldn't keep my eyes open and I got into bed for a few minutes. I was there until four, dreaming wild things about the missus who was suffering because of the German at the mental hospital. My dream was so vivid that when I woke up I couldn't free myself from these worries, to the point that I kept seeing the German in a top hat and frock coat, and the missus with white plaster on her face. I tossed and turned in my poncho, jumped out of bed, and said aloud, "I have to see her. There's not a Reger nor a Campolongo in the world who can stop me." I was a little stupefied, afraid that the women could hear me. They're going to say that I'm crazy, I thought. What do I care?

XXVI

To rouse myself I had some *maté*, because if I wasn't careful, that nightmare about the doctors would go on again, like a movie in my head, getting more and more disagreeable when the missus appeared with the plaster.

Then, at Incas Street, I took the 113 bus. I got off at the bridge, turned right, walked to the corner of Baigorria and San Martín Avenue. There I hung around, posted behind the trees. In my eagerness to catch sight of Diana, I didn't think about the passers-by who, I guess, must have eyed me with suspicion. I won't deny that I had a scare when Dr. Campolongo himself came out of the building, crossed the street, and went right toward me. I quickly hid behind an old abandoned truck and watched the doctor go over to the newsstand and buy a package of cigarettes.

Another climactic moment was when I caught a glimpse of a woman in a window on the fifth floor of the institute. Without the slightest hesitation I said to myself, It's Diana. I've always believed that if one day I'm dead and buried and Diana steps on my grave, I'll recognize her. The window opened: what I had taken for Diana, why deny it, was a rather fat nurse.

Before going home I took 113 to Pampa and Estomba Streets, because I decided to pass by the dog school. In the lodge only one very weak, yellowish light was on. I stood guard a half hour, pacing back and forth; from time to time I glanced sideways toward the little light. I swear that if a patrolman came by, he would have asked me for identification, and if some friend saw me, he'd think that putting the missus away had driven me crazy; I'm not that far gone, but at this rate, I'm close enough.

Back home I found Martincito crouching behind my

father-in-law's wheelbarrow which, in Don Martín's dreams of grandeur, he had bought to work in the garden. Puzzled, I asked him, "What are you doing?"

He seemed annoyed and signaled me to go away. As I hesitated, he explained.

"If you stay around, the enemy will catch me."

When I saw the neighbor's boy, a pale fat kid, dragging himself like a worm, I suspected that they were playing war. I was going to smile at Martincito, but he looked so irritated that I withdrew in good form.

XXVII

I stayed awake all night again. I heard Aldini's cock at dawn, and in the morning, when I went to have my *maté*, the kid had gone to school and I had to put up with Adriana María's repartee.

"A good thing," she said, "that he doesn't lose sleep over his little wife."

What do we know about people? Nothing.

In the afternoon the foreman from the factory came, paid the agreed sum, and took away the clock.

It seems incredible: after a while I couldn't control myself and I went off on my customary round of the mental hospital and the school. Because one is always bumping into the same loafers, I met Fats Picardo on Estomba Street.

"What are you doing here?" he said.

To confuse him I asked, "Did you change stamping grounds?"

"If I were you," Picardo advised me, "I wouldn't look for trouble with the German. He's a mean guy."

"What trouble am I looking for?"

In the most casual manner he answered, "You know what I mean."

I quickly invented a story to explain what I was doing on Estomba Street.

"You're not going to believe me," I said, because one tends to show people what one's thinking, "but I thought I'd give the missus a surprise."

"You don't say," he remarked, as if he didn't believe me. "What kind of surprise?"

"A dog, of course," I said. "The missus always wanted a dog. It's a well-known fact. Ask anyone who knows her. Now I'm going to indulge her."

Picardo smiled and looked at me.

Speaking in a solemn tone that probably intimidated him, I said, "I want her to make a grand entrance."

He mumbled, "You musn't have great faith in yourself if you need the support of a dog."

I pretended I hadn't heard. I asked him, "What did you say?"

"Where are you getting the money?"

"Here." I touched my wallet. Then I added, as if giving myself important airs, "They brought me the clock from the Lorenzutti factory to fix."

For a moment I stopped him short, but he reacted.

"Instead of investing in dogs," he said, "pay me what you owe me."

"I don't owe you anything."

"The eighty tickets I played for you."

"I told you over and over again that I don't bet."

"Don't do that to me and don't shout. The doctor is favorably impressed because I sold you the tickets. If you pay me with your winnings, what does it matter to you?"

Lately Picardo has become very insistent.

XXVIII

Half a block away I looked back and saw Picardo watching me from the corner without trying to hide it. Because of that pain in the neck, I said to myself, even though I don't want to, I have to go in.

There was such a smell of dogs in the office that I pitied Diana, as if I was sure she was living there.

The jealous man cannot stay good-natured for long. When I realized the scope of what I had thought, I started looking for traces of the missus with a bitterness that amazed me. Of course I didn't find them. You might say that if I distrust her so easily I mustn't love her very much. On that point you're wrong, although for my part maybe I don't know how to give convincing reasons.

The buck-toothed guy who works there appeared.

"What do you want?" he asked.

From his manner of speaking, you would place him somewhere between human and animal.

"To talk to Standle," I said.

The boy opened the door halfway and announced, "Someone to see you."

He didn't take his eyes off me or go away until Standle came. The German was visibly annoyed, but immediately hid it with his silly expression. I remember as if it were this moment that I couldn't help wondering if the man were hiding something or if he'd done me a bad turn.

"What are you looking for?" he asked.

Perhaps to study his reactions I said the following:

"I'm looking for a dog to give to Diana, when she comes home."

"Missus Diana?"

I swear I caught a sarcastic expression in his eyes and mouth. It made me angry and I asked, "Who else could it be?"

Showing a lively business sense he moved on to the subject of the deal.

"At this moment, you'll notice a real decrease in supply," he said. "The first effect on the market is the rise of prices."

"I figured as much," I answered.

"What you need is a bitch."

"Or a male dog."

"A male can get carried away with a bitch. A bitch won't be distracted from her duty."

I warned him:

"I've heard that story already."

"Come with me. I'll show you what you need."

He opened the door and we walked between two rows of kennels. It's not that I'm fussy but I swear the place didn't seem hospitable. All that barking and the smell of dogs mixed with disinfectant depressed and saddened me. It made me feel like forgetting the whole operation.

"See that pretty young one over there?" the German said.

She was a very pretty German shepherd. When we came over, she was lying with her head flat against the floor and from down there she looked up at us with attentive, golden eyes. She seemed amused, as if sharing a joke with us, and in a second she switched from lying still to jumping and playing around. I swear I thought, I'll take her. As Ceferina often says, it's hard to resist beauty. A bad comparison, of course, because Ceferina is referring to the missus.

"How much are you asking?"

"A hundred dollars," he answered.

"That's outrageous."

It was an outrage, but it also was (and this seemed more important to me) the same amount that I had received for the Lorenzutti Ausonia. I realized that if I spent that money on a dog for the missus, it might turn the bad luck into good luck. It goes without saying that while I was thinking all this, the German spoke nonstop. I think he was praising the animal's intelligence and capricious nature. In a squeaky voice he exclaimed, "A woman after all! But gentle, good, and a capital point, very advanced in the training course."

"What's her name?" I asked.

Again he seemed annoyed. Courageously he assured me, "I suspect that you'll like the name."

"Why?"

"She's the missus' namesake."

When I understood, I was upset. Coming home with a bitch named Diana was not wise, because there would be no way of saving her from the women's ill feelings and bad treatment.

In that first moment I reasoned calmly.

"She's no good. What else can you offer?"

He showed me a half dozen dogs. The comparison was impossible.

"Cute pups, but it's no use," he stated. "The gentleman chose right from the beginning. Love at first sight."

I looked at him with respect because he was right. From the moment I saw her, I was attracted to Diana.

"I'll take her," I said.

"Congratulations," Standle said.

He shook my hand till it hurt.

I know perfectly well that I behaved like a child. Since they put the missus away I haven't been myself.

XXIX

As soon as we came into the alley I saw lame Aldini stationed with Naughty Boy. Though it seems incredible,

Diana took a lively interest in that sickly animal and she just about dragged me over to him. While the dogs studied and got to know each other, I talked to Aldini.

"What's this?" he asked.

"A bitch," I answered.

"Where'd you get her?"

"I just bought her."

Aldini made one of those polite remarks which even today distinguish him as the gentleman he is, although he no longer wears the white bow tie of his youth, when he'd invite the gang of kids (you and I included) to go to the soccer match. With one magical word he picked up my spirits.

"Congratulations!"

I stood there looking at him gratefully and was slow to figure out what he was now saying. Aldini repeated:

"What's her name?"

A while before the German had seemed uncomfortable at the question; now it was my turn to be uncomfortable.

"Pure chance," I assured him.

"What?" he asked, opening his eyes wide.

"It's as if they thought I'd forget the missus."

Recovering his poise, he smiled.

"Don't tell me her name is Diana."

"You're quick," I said sincerely.

"Where'd you get her?" he asked again.

"I bought her from Standle."

Aldini came at me with a barrage of questions about the animal's origins, which I didn't answer for lack of knowledge. I admit that for a moment I felt disillusioned; while I was thinking, The family-tree craze applied to dogs, he concluded his questions with the alarming words, "I hope she won't bring you any trouble."

I immediately reacted.

"Why would she do that?"

"To keep a full stock, in that school they pick up stray dogs when they're not stealing them from their very homes."

"Impossible," I said.

"Impossible?" he repeated, getting worked up. "One day you're very cheerfully taking your new Diana for a walk and the first passerby stops you with the claim that the dog is his and that you stole her."

"I bought her in good faith."

"You'll have to prove it."

"I won't give her back even if they take me down to the police station."

"You have every right. Let me add an encouraging opinion: according to a friend of mine who owns a greyhound, they don't steal dogs that they sell to private individuals."

"I'm a private individual."

"It's to your advantage," he said, and he lowered his voice to add, "They steal dogs which no human being will ever see again."

"What dogs are those?"

"The ones they deliver to laboratories."

"What for?"

"What do you mean what for? Don't you know? For vivisection!"

Again I heard the word vivisection, which I hadn't remembered until I heard it in my dreams those other nights.

"What's their purpose?" I asked.

"The same as always. Greed. Money is horrible."

"I think money brings bad luck," I said, to see if I could get some enlightening opinion out of him.

Maybe he didn't hear me because he was thinking about something that worried him. Holding me by the shoulders, he murmured, "Between you and me, I don't think Standle sincerely loves dogs."

XXX

At home they received me better than I expected. Martincito jumped with joy and played with the dog; he seemed happy. I remember saying to myself, He's a wonderful boy. As for the women, from the first they were against her. Ceferina pretended not to understand why I had brought the dog.

"Didn't I tell you that hawkeye was out looking for a replacement for my sister?" Adriana María asked. "Of course, out of respect, he brought back her namesake."

Sometimes I wonder if she really loves the missus.

Ceferina warned me that she wasn't going to clean up the animal's mess.

"For that go find yourself some native girl from the provinces," she said, as if she were an English lady.

The days passed; the dog didn't mess up the house and Ceferina's annoyance grew. I wonder if some women don't need vexations and quarrels to live in peace. A good thing she didn't think of blaming me (which she could have had reason to do) for taking time from the clocks to train the dog. When she looked at us during training time, believe me, her face was the very picture of contempt. If the dog disobeyed me, she'd use any pretext to pet her and even to give her a lump of sugar. The fact that I took her out for a walk several times a day unleashed, God knows why, the greatest indignation.

"Have you gotten yourself some girlfriend in the neighborhood or do you really like to take the dog for a walk?" my sister-in-law asked me.

I answered, "Of course I like to. What's wrong with that?"

"Maybe you're some kind of degenerate, huh?"

"You, my dear," Old Ceferina—who, if angered,

defends me—joined in, "could, from time to time, wash that filthy mind of yours."

Strong emotions make me feel close to the dog. When I see her black, refined snout, her golden eyes, so expressively intelligent and devoted, I can't help loving her. Maybe Ceferina was right when she said I'm a lover of beauty. There is something about this point that worries me: the beauty I like is physical beauty. If I think of the attraction I feel for this dog, I say to myself, With Diana, the missus, the same thing occurs. Don't I adore in her, above all, that unique face, those deep and marvelous eyes, the color of her skin and hair, the shape of her body, of her hands, and that smell in which I could lose myself forever with my eyes closed?

The presence of an animal changes our lives. As if I had suffered hunger and thirst for a total love—such was, I swear, what this dog offered me—from the moment I took her home I felt in such good company that I got to wondering if I weren't missing Diana less. I suspect that these doubts were only another proof of the tendency to brood which I had developed. I missed Diana as anxiously as ever, but the dog, with her devotion, how shall I say, made me more stable.

At the moment things are happening we don't give them their due. Ever since I've had a dog, I look at the other dogs on the street and, if I see them twice—you're going to laugh—I recognize them. Among those of us who walk dogs, we easily strike up friendships. We're what you call a large family. My sister-in-law claims that if a woman is expecting, or afraid that she is, everywhere she goes she runs into big bellies. As far as I'm concerned, ever since I have Diana, all I meet is people with dogs. Or dogs who come over to me. For example, the other afternoon, in Chas Park, a pointer bitch, with big eyes and a sad expression—tormented, I should say—jumped on top of me, as if she knew me. With a courage that filled me with pride, Diana chased her away. Then we ran into the bucktoothed guy from the school; I wonder who that fool thinks he is: he pretended he didn't see us.

If Martincito weren't so friendly to the dog, I wouldn't have dared to go out and leave her alone with the women in the house. I could count on the boy; he took care of and played with her to the extent that I sometimes wondered if he wasn't stealing her affection away from me. Diana preferred Martincito's game to spending hours lying at my feet in the shop. Probably the smell of the kerosene heater bothered her. We should always remember that dogs, Ceferina explained to me, are superior to human beings in matters of smell.

Really, my fear that the boy would steal such total affection away from me must have been rather ridiculous. By the way she looked at me, I should have realized that the dog loved me. I don't think anybody has eyes like that.

XXXI

With all that walking and training, I got behind on my work. To meet my deadlines with the customers, I had no choice but to go back to the shop at night. Instead of the television, a broken mainspring or spindle, a gear with some worn-down cog, kept me busy till dawn.

One night I had Mr. Pedroso's Longines spread out in front of me. Pedroso, you remember, is the guy who's retired from Mariano Acha's funeral parlor. To begin putting it back together, I picked up the first piece with the pincers when I thought — you're going to think this is the fantasy of a perturbed man, because I didn't hear the slightest sound and Diana, who barks at anything, really didn't wake up—that someone was spying on me. Without dropping the pincers, I very slowly turned my head and, framed in the window facing the garden, I saw for a second or two a very white, closely shaven face. I'll bet you don't know what I quickly thought? That to work at night in these times, a watchmaker like myself, surrounded by things of value which don't belong to him, should bring a weapon to the shop, and that the Eibar revolver with the mother-of-pearl handle, which I inherited from my father, was in the bedroom bureau, far from my hand. Immediately, some action began. The dog barked, I dropped the pincers, and when I went to open the door, there was a knock. There was a man in the dark, whom the dog tried to avoid. It was the bucktooth guy. He hugged her, held her, said to her:

"How are you, Diana?" Bucky gave me a training collar and explained, "It's from Standle."

Then I started thinking that maybe his pal with the pale face had stayed outside and that Bucky was purposely holding Diana down so that she wouldn't go after him.

I'm going to admit something that I'm ashamed of: ever since the missus left, my nerves have been bad. The appearance of the face in the window and the conversation with Bucky, which was as normal as can be left me without any desire to work. As I went to bed, I thought that I wouldn't fall asleep easily. I was upset all night long, because I dreamed that the pale man had stolen my dog. In the nightmare, my legs tired from walking so much, I anxiously looked for the dog all over the neighborhood and Chas Park. I called to her mentally and I believe, God forgive me, that in my anguish I confused and even identified one Diana with the other. Believe you me, I woke up a wreck. Seeing the dog lying on the scatter rug, I patted her head.

I took a shower, dressed, and as I was going into the

kitchen to have some *maté*, I heard the old lady saying to my sister-in-law, "Lucho is a child of circumstances."

How do you like these phrases she thinks up? Adriana María, apparently, understood her and agreed. I left the *maté* for later and took the dog out for a walk.

In the alley I met Aldini. The fact that each of us has a dog has strengthened our old friendship.

"This morning I saw Picardo," he said to me. "He was so spruced up and conceited that he didn't say hello. Incredible."

I thought, My horse won and he kept the money.

To change the subject I couldn't think of anything better to say than, "You won't believe what I saw outside the shop window last night."

I told him about the appearance of the pale face and the bucktoothed boy.

"Standle sold you the dog," he said, "and now he wants to steal her for the laboratory. You're going to have to keep your eyes peeled."

Swept away by real indignation I said, "I let them take away one Diana, but I'm not going to let them take the other."

I realized on the spot that if I had said those words in front of Adriana María or Ceferina, I would have been open to all kinds of jokes. Aldini, who's just as intelligent as the women, let it pass.

Then we got into loftier subjects. In the hopes of understanding my affection for Diana through his affection for Elvira, I said, "I'm going to ask you a stupid question. Can you tell me who's the person you love most?"

He answered, "Well, you know, Elvira."

His answer convinced me that we could understand each other. In my eagerness to reach that goal, I didn't really worry about being tactful and I presented him with a second question.

"What do you love most about Elvira?"

Even his double chin blushed bright red. After a while he said something which filled me with amazement.

"Maybe one loves the image he has."

"I don't follow you," I admitted.

"I'm lucky in that Elvira never contradicts that image."

"Good. If I love Diana physically, perhaps I'm not so wrong. Perhaps Diana is no less her physical self than Elvira the image you have of her. One doesn't have to dig so deep."

Aldini answered, very matter-of-fact, "You're too intelligent for me."

I don't think I'm more intelligent than other people, but I've thought a lot about certain subjects.

XXXII

One afternoon at siesta time I dreamed that nonsense again. You're going to laugh: I dreamed that I was in my bed, in my room, and that Diana was sleeping next to me, down below on the scatter rug. Exactly what was happening in real life, except that in the dream I spoke to her. I asked her, I remember, what her soul was like and I said, "It's certainly more generous than that of many women." You understand, without openly naming them, I was referring to my sister-in-law and Ceferina. I asked the dog to speak to me, because if not, I said to her, I would never know the soul that was looking at me from those deep eyes. Screams awakened me. For reasons which I knew in the dream, but which very soon were erased from my mind, I awoke grieving, with a real need to be with the missus. I heard Adriana María's voice, which reached me loud and clear. I figured it was coming from the kitchen and wondered if I had heard the old lady's voice too. When I went there, hoping to have a *maté*, I had the unpleasant experience of finding the two women locked in an argument. I thought that I had been unfair, particularly insensitive, to my sister-in-law. If I looked at her suddenly, I could take her for the missus, except for her hair color.

Then they say that there's such a thing as extra-sensory perception. While I was abandoning myself to such favorable thoughts of her, Adriana María was hatching a grudge against me that didn't take long to explode. I didn't bother about the women until they raised their voices and practically screamed. This didn't surprise me, because a day rarely passes when they aren't screaming at or insulting each other. If I could reason more quickly, I would have withdrawn, but as I'm slow-moving, before understanding anything I felt the stupid obligation to patch things up.

I then had the proof that I should keep my lips sealed and not speak about matters that are important to me in front of persons ready to interpret what I say with ill feelings. On several occasions I commented at home on the latest episodes and the thoughts I had about them. Vaguely I must have thought that these women, after all, were my family and that if I can't comment to anybody on the worries I have, I am very alone.

When they told me why they were fighting, they tightened the knot which was holding me there. Ceferina explained.

"For treating Elvira, the doctors presented poor Aldini with what you could call one hell of a bill."

"The cripple doesn't earn a red cent," Adriana María cut in, "because not I or anybody in his right mind is going to take furniture to a senile old man to be fixed. You know what he's good for? For walking the dog."

I would say that she looked at me suggestively.

"He's not so old. Only ten or twelve years older than me," I protested.

"Elvira's illness ate up all his savings," Ceferina said.

"He deserves it for being stingy and reactionary," Adriana María said.

"What does that have to do with it?" I asked.

"What do you mean what does it have to do with it? He doesn't contribute to the pension funds!"

Ceferina herself admitted, "The worst possible crime."

"If I just say the word to Social Security they'll put him behind bars. He doesn't contribute to the retirement funds nor did he ever take the simple precaution to join the Spanish Social Club."

I argued, "He's from Italian stock."

"Then he can't complain," my sister-in-law pronounced.

The women started raising Cain again and I thought of the lesson Aldini had given me. Without a thought I had used him as a shoulder to cry on, but he never bothered me with troubles and complaints. Unfortunately, it was too late for me to follow that great example of good behavior, because there were no longer many left in the neighborhood who hadn't heard about my problems.

Adriana María commented, "Aldini may have gotten into debt to cure his wife, but the one he really loves is the dog."

I thought she said "the filthy dog." I protested with a dignity that I was the first to applaud.

"As far as that's concerned I don't think you're being either fair or reasonable."

Shouldn't have said it. She whipped around like a mainspring, pinned her flashing eyes on me, and asked, "How dare you say the word 'reasonable'?" For a while she mumbled furiously, "Some nerve he has. I don't know why they don't lock him up in the institute. I swear I'm going to turn him in."

Without being intimidated I said, "Don't confuse sadness with madness."

"You're sad because you're mad."

I sincerely admitted, "I don't follow you."

As if she had memorized a lesson, maybe to recite it before a committee of doctors, she began the enumeration of charges.

"If you listen to him, the same people who sold him the dog are going to steal her from him."

Like an idiot I explained, "The idea never, even remotely, occurred to me! Aldini put me on my guard."

"What do the old man's opinions have to do with it? Birds of a feather flock together. Now this one is imitating him and, so as not to be different, he brings home a dog that has the same name as his little wife."

When I heard that about my "little wife" it seemed impossible that minutes before I had looked at her with affection. In some way I'm disturbed and even disgusted by the idea that a highly attractive and familiar body, because it's identical to the missus', hides such a different soul. Adriana María continued.

"He chose the dog because that was her name. Or maybe he himself gave it to her. Sometimes I wonder if what he likes about my sister is her name."

Eager to keep myself within the strictest truth, I admitted, "There's nothing ugly about it."

For the first time Adriana María smiled.

"If you'd like to call me Diana," she said as if some thought amused her, "I'm not against it."

I thought it necessary to make this point quite clear.

"Your name is Adriana María."

"On the other hand the dog's name is Diana and he's nuts about her. You're not going to tell me that it's not strange for a husband to love only his legitimate wife. When that wife is my sister, I have every right to believe that that man is not normal."

"You don't have the right," I protested.

Boy, you should have heard her.

"The gentleman denies me the right. Since when am I

going to ask permission from a madman who sees pale faces in the window at night?"

"I swear I saw it."

"Who cares what the ignoramus saw? I'm going to tell the whole thing to those doctors, so they can see how ignorant and crazy you are. Only a madman imagines that the doctors in the mental hospital, God knows for what horrible reason, lock up people in their right minds. I'm not going to turn you in out of mere spite, but to protect myself."

Upset, I asked, "To protect yourself?"

"Yes, to protect myself," she answered. "You're a malicious nut, who's trying to steal my own son's affection away from me."

"Don't twist things around."

"Who are you to speak to me in that manner?"

"Martincito and I are great friends, but I never tried to steal his affection away from you."

"What, do you take me for a fool or something? You listen: the boy tells me everything. Behind my back you praise my sister and attack me. You try to separate us."

"You're slandering me."

"I'm warning you: I'm going to bring my old man up-to-date, in detail, and he's going to knock your block off."

"God help him," I said, and I petted Diana.

Adriana María started crying.

"Now you're threatening," she said between sobs. "I'm leaving with Martincito. I thought I would stay in this house forever."

94

XXXIII

Maybe I don't know how to deal with women. If I looked at her silently, my sister-in-law said that I was making fun of her suffering, and if I asked her to calm down, she'd say that she couldn't stand hypocrites.

I went to my room, put all the money I'd made recently in my pocket—out of pure laziness I didn't put it in the bank—and I went out with the dog. Luckily, Aldini was in the alley. I asked him, "Do you think it's right for friends to keep secrets from each other?"

"Secrets, no, but neither is it a matter of telling everything, like women and the queers nowadays."

"Do you think it's right for you to pay the doctor's bills, without saying a word to me?"

"Why should I advertise it?"

"Because at this moment, it so happens, I can help you."

When I put my hand in my pocket, he stopped me.

"You shouldn't show your money on the street."

We went in. Limping arduously he led me to his room. Elvira was in the kitchen.

I repeated, "At this moment, it so happens, I can help you. It's scary to say so: the money's pouring in on me."

I felt as if I were bragging.

"Maybe tomorrow you'll need it," Aldini said simply.

"In that case I'll ask you for it."

"How the devil am I going to return it? These days the man who's out of work is like a pocket with a hole in it."

I gave him the bundle.

"Don't you think you're making a mistake?" he asked. "Because of your situation—I don't know if you get my meaning."

He counted the money and insisted on giving me a

receipt. Then it was necessary to accept Elvira's *maté* and to have a polite conversation.

I left, satisfied. After a while I wondered if I hadn't lent Aldini the money out of the simple desire to look like a great friend and like a generous man. Or even worse: if I hadn't lent it to him because I thought that money was bad luck. As you see, the missus is right: interested in myself only, I question and scrutinize myself to the point where I forget about other people. Shall I tell you the truth? I was afraid that this whole thing would bring me bad luck.

As I don't know how to attend to two things at the same time, it took me a while to notice that there was a car in front of the house. It was a taxi that Adriana María had loaded with suitcases and dresses on hangers. My sister-in-law rejected me when I made a gesture to help her and, without worrying if the driver could hear her, she snapped at me with hate.

"Heartless jerk."

I would have put the things into the car anyway, if it hadn't been for Martincito, who opened and closed his eyes, moved his hands as if they were dog ears, made faces, and stuck his tongue out at me. Even though you may think I'm a weak man, I'll admit that Martincito's attitude deeply affected me. When they left, Ceferina said to me, "Don't eat your heart out."

"Easily said."

"She must have found a man. There are women like that. Before doing what they feel like doing, they blame someone else."

I was upset by the commotion, my sister-in-law's parting, and especially the kid's mockery. Sorrowfully I said to myself that I should lose all hopes that Ceferina, or anybody, could understand me. The old lady hugged me for awhile, until she let go to look at me with joy, with tenderness, and (I will add, because I'm an ungrateful wretch) with ferocity. I believe she said, "Alone at last!"

XXXIV

Although my sister-in-law's departure definitely meant a relief, my life continued its anguished obstacle course. This consisted mainly of telephone calls from Don Martín's house; father and daughter passed the phone to one another, taking turns to shout threats and obscene words at me.

Finally, on the afternoon of December 5, Reger Samaniego called and left a message for me to please come to the mental hospital. Ceferina, who took the message, didn't think it necessary to ask for explanations.

I imagined the worst calamities, so that I went off like a shot and arrived immediately, more dead than alive. I was sweating so much that it was embarrassing. As if I were dreaming the same nightmare again, at first everything happened like the last time. Dr. Campolongo received me in person in Reger Samaniego's office; he locked the door and held out to me, very courteously, a pale hand as wet as mine but markedly cooler.

"Do you have wings?" he asked.

I looked at him not understanding what he meant. In my mental confusion I suspected that he took me for a nut.

"I don't understand," I said.

"I'd barely hung up and you're already here."

I noticed that his face—shaven, rather round—was unusually pale.

"Dr. Reger Samaniego wants to speak to you," he said. "Will you wait a minute?"

I said yes, but I had to hold myself back so as not to add that the minute should please not be too long because I was very nervous. To keep myself busy I compared Campolongo's face to the one I caught at the shop window the other night. Campolongo's was equally pale but rounder.

The doctor went into the inner office. I remembered some of Adriana María's threats and wondered if I hadn't fallen into a trap.

After a while the same door opened, a nurse came in, I stood up, she told me to sit down.

"The doctor will be with you shortly," she assured me.

She was dark-haired, with a very pointy chin and shining eyes as if she had a fever. She leaned on the arm of my chair and, looking at me close up, asked, "Would you like some coffee? A magazine to keep you busy while you're all alone?"

I said no. She smiled as if to mean that she was sorry about my answer and left.

I suddenly imagined that the doctor had called me there with the intention of getting me away from home. While I sit waiting here, the German and the guy with bushy eyebrows are going to my house to steal my dog, I thought.

My nerves were just about out of control when Reger Samaniego appeared. He was tall, thin, had a sharp nose. Maybe because of his face, shadowed by a three- or four-day beard, I compared him to a wolf. I wondered if I would bring bad luck by thinking about that nonsense and not Diana. Reger Samaniego started talking before I could pay attention. When I finally heard him, he was saying, "She's changed. Don't expect her to be the same. She's changed for the better."

I said nothing, because I didn't know what to answer;

finally I said to him, "I almost prefer her to be the same."

"She's the same, but she's better."

My answer didn't express disbelief, but rather hope.

Reger Samaniego continued, "If the maximum percentage of illness were one hundred, at what percentile would you figure the missus' ailment?"

"I don't understand a word you're saying," I said.

"Would you place the missus' illness at twenty, thirty, or forty percent?"

"Let's say twenty."

"Let's say twenty, but it was really double that. Now we've lowered it to zero. Or, to say it the other way around, we've raised the missus' psychological health to one hundred percent."

"Is she well?"

I was also going to ask him if he would give her back to me soon, but before I decided to speak, he answered my first question.

"Completely well. Please, try now to follow my reasoning. She was—I don't want to offend you, please understand—the rotten apple of your marriage. Do you follow me?"

"I follow you."

"When the missus wasn't well, she made you ill."

In strange situations, so as not to act like a coward, perhaps one must be very brave. I felt like escaping. Assuming a carefree tone, I said to him, "For all I know, Doctor, they've been catching you off guard and telling you fibs. I'm perfectly fine."

"I asked you, Mr. Bordenave, to try to follow me. Don't answer if you don't understand."

I answered, "I understand you. But I'm perfectly fine. Believe me. Perfect."

He seemed to me to have ants in his veins. In the most imperturbably slow manner, Reger Samaniego went on with his explanation.

"The rotten apple infects the rest of the fruit bowl. The missus, to a certain degree, has infected you."

The explanation, as I had foreseen, was taking a dangerous turn. To show my sanity and good spirits I asked him, "To what percent?"

"I don't understand," he said.

"Five percent?"

"Let's not get into percentages," he answered, visibly annoyed, "which are completely made up anyway. Let's say, instead, that now, with the missus coming home in good health, you will be playing the role of the rotten apple."

"What should I do?" I asked in a faint voice.

I closed my eyes, because I was sure of hearing the feared words "you should be put away." I heard:

"Watch yourself."

"Watch myself?" I asked, confused but relieved.

"Of course. Repress your inclination to make her sick again."

Perhaps because I thought I was safe or perhaps because I was really offended, I protested.

"How could you possibly think that I would have an inclination to make Diana sick?"

"Remember what I'm saying to you. You can, without meaning to, I don't doubt it, unchain the illness again. Do you want the missus to have a relapse?"

I succeeded in repeating, "How could you possibly think that?"

"Then promise me that you're not going to long for habits, or a certain way of acting, that the missus might have forgotten?"

I assured him, "I don't understand."

He hid his face in his hands. When he parted them, he seemed very tired.

"I'm going to make a bad comparison, to see if I can help you. A man who had bought the milkman's horse complained because the animal stopped in front of every door. He took it to another man, so that he'd get rid of that bad habit and, when it was returned to him, he complained because the horse didn't stop anywhere."

Getting angry just in case, I answered, "I don't understand the comparison."

"I have the greatest respect for the missus," he assured me. "I seized upon the comparison in the hope, with the perhaps absurd illusion, that you would understand me. I repeat: the missus is changed and I hope that you will not complain."

"Why should I complain?"

"One misses the good and the bad."

"What can I do?"

He said the following words which I will never forget.

"I'm telling you, don't push her back to the kind of life she had when she was sick." He again covered his face with his hands and then looked upward, with the expression of a person contemplating something wonderful. "Perhaps a trip, a change of residence would be good, but I don't mean to get you into further expense. The ideal solution, do you want me to tell you what the ideal solution would have been?"

I swear I answered, "No."

I spoke in such a low voice that he must not have heard me. He continued.

"To put you away as well!"

At that moment his face seemed narrower and pointier to me. A real wolf face. It was pale, but his unshaven beard darkened it.

"That would be a waste of money," I complained, as if I didn't think much of what he was saying.

"Back to the apples," he answered. "If one mate gets sick, the marriage gets sick. You will prove to me that you are healthy only if you don't push the missus back to her old habits."

"I promise," I said.

He covered his face again, and suddenly he slapped the brass turtle that was on the desk. I was startled, because it was a very loud bell.

Campolongo appeared. The director asked him, "Is Mrs. Bordenave ready?"

The other took his time in answering.

"She's ready."

Finally the director ordered, "Bring her in." Despite my confusion I realized that Reger was giving a useless explanation. "They've come to take her home."

I couldn't believe my ears, but my happiness ended suddenly when I saw that Reger took out of the pocket of his smock an unmistakable piece of paper. Because I don't have the money, now they're not going to give her back to me, I thought. Maybe if I called old Aldini on the phone, or if I went back to his house right away, I could recover the money I lent.

"I didn't think of bringing money..." I murmured.

That didn't seem to me to be a very convincing excuse, but the words which Reger Samaniego said were even more incredible.

"Pay me when you can."

He gave me the piece of paper, rubbed his hands together, and with the air of a hypocritical businessman he added, "My little bill."

I examined it, again I couldn't believe it and turned the sheet around to see if it continued on the other side. It didn't.

"That's all?" I asked.

"That's all," he answered.

"But, Doctor, that doesn't even pay for the food."

To myself I was saying, With what I have in the bank it's more than enough for me.

"Don't worry," Reger Samaniego answered.

"There's no reason for you to be doing charity."

"There's no reason for you to worry too much," he answered. It took me time to realize that he was no longer talking about the bill. "If, unwillingly, of course, you feel inclined to reproduce the former situation, don't worry, there will always be someone to inform me"—at that point he hit his chest to indicate, perhaps, that I could depend on him—"and I will have you put away immediately, without that implying, for you, exorbitant expense."

I was deep in the most depressing thoughts when I heard the cry:

"Lucho!"

With open arms, golden, rosy, beautiful, Diana ran toward me. I had the presence of mind to think, She's happy because she sees me. I will never forget this proof of love.

XXXV

With my right hand I gripped Diana's arm, with my left her suitcase, we were leaving the institute, going home; I felt I was the happiest man in the world. In that extraordinary moment we spoke of trivial things, until after awhile Diana asked me how her father was and if he was mad at me for having put her away.

"Quite a bit," I said.

"We'll try to make him be reasonable." She started laughing and asked me, "Was Adriana María after you?"

"I don't understand."

"She's wild about you!"

There's no doubt about it: women are sharper than we are.

While I walked, holding her by the arm, believe you

me I had a strong desire to kiss her. You'll wonder if I lost my sense of decency. Believe me, I'm not telling you these intimate things for the pleasure of airing them, but because I think they can be meaningful to the understanding of the mysterious and extraordinary events that happened afterward. So that you don't think I was a bit crazy or even just not myself, as Adriana María spread around in conversations with people in the alley and even in the neighborhood, it's good for you to know my mood when I returned home. I would describe it as the simple happiness of a man who has just been reunited with his wife after a long separation.

We were going along those blessed streets so distracted by our conversation and by the pleasure of being together that we didn't notice that we were back home.

"I've got a big surprise for you," I announced.

"Tell me what it is," she answered.

"Think a little. Something you always wanted."

"Don't make me think," she said, "I'm feeling very dumb. I don't have any idea."

"I bought you a dog."

She hugged me. I took her hand and led her through the little garden gate. Diana came out to greet us. Though the dog is distrustful with strangers, you should have seen how quickly they made friends.

"What's her name?" she asked.

"Guess," I said. "A name that's very familiar to you."

"I don't have any idea."

"The most familiar of all."

After a while she asked, "Don't tell me that her name is Diana?"

"Is that why I love her so much?"

"So they named you Diana too, huh?" she asked the dog, while she petted her. "Poor little thing."

She went into the house looking at everything, and when Ceferina appeared she hugged her, which was very moving.

"Dinner will be ready in a half hour," said Ceferina. "Why don't you go to your room and take the things out of your suitcase?"

Diana said to me, "Stay with me."

I took her by the hand, led her to the room. Everything amazed her, she stopped at every step, she seemed to hesitate, I think she trembled a little. Unwillingly, I asked her, "Did you have a very bad time?"

"I don't want to remember. I want to be happy."

I hugged her and began kissing her. Her heart beat loudly against my chest.

She sat on the edge of the bed, like a little girl, and began to undress.

"I'm in my home, with my husband," she said. "I want to forget the rest and be happy with you."

What I'm going to tell you is embarrassing: I cried with gratitude. In some way I was living the moment I had always waited for. I had been with Diana other times and I had been very happy with her, but I had never heard such a clear expression of love from her. I hugged her, held her against me, kissed her, believe me, till I bit her. I was so blind that I didn't realize that Diana was crying. I asked her:

"Is anything wrong? Did I hurt you?"

"No, no," she said. "I'm the one who should ask you to forgive me, because it was my fault you suffered. Now I'm going to be good. I only want to be happy with you."

As she insisted on her guilt, I ended up saying that I had always loved her. She's going to answer back, I thought, that I'm already beginning to scold her again. She looked at me with those extraordinary eyes and asked me:

"Are you sure you're not going to miss my short-comings?"

I couldn't help suspecting that Reger Samaniego had warned her against my so-called inclination to push her again toward madness.

"I'm going to love you even more," I said.

"Are you going to love me if I'm yours completely?"

I kissed her hands, I thanked her. I didn't kneel down before her because Ceferina opened the door and said in her shrill voice:

"If you don't finish up here soon, the soufflé is going to fall flat."

I commented to Diana, "What an unpleasant woman."

"It's jealousy," Diana explained, laughing. "Don't pay any attention."

For some reason I said to myself at that moment, How strange. Today, while talking to Reger Samaniego, I didn't even think that Diana might be furious with me because I hadn't prevented them from putting her away. If they had returned her to me as she'd been, now she would surely be torturing me with reproaches and reprimands. Reger's right. She's changed. She's cured.

XXXVI

A few days later, on the corner of Carbajal and Thunder Street, I bumped into Dr. Reger Samaniego. I was so absentminded that when I saw him I was startled. It's true that without the black shadow of his poorly shaven beard his face, because of its whiteness, looked like that of a corpse.

"What a big hurry to pay," he said to me.

"I don't like debts," I answered.

I think that the very afternoon they returned Diana to me, I had gone to the mental hospital to pay the bill.

"And the prodigal daughter?" he asked.

"I don't understand," I answered.

"You never change," he said in an unpleasant little tone.

"I still don't understand," I assured him.

"How's the missus?"

"There are no complaints."

These words made me ashamed, because I felt mean. It seemed to me that I owed the doctor a lot and that only out of frankly gratuitous misgivings and pigheadedness did I answer him that way. Of course, Diana didn't give me any reason to complain. Things were going so well with her that I sometimes wondered if everything would end in some catastrophe. Life has taught me that when things are generally too good, they don't foreshadow anything good at all; besides, I'm a bit superstitious. No one really would have qualified Diana's behavior as strange; I obviously was surprised because I wasn't accustomed to her being so affectionate and well-behaved. I'm not exaggerating: Diana left me in charge of all decisions, so that in time I had to convince myself that in our house I was the master. As you'll remember, the doctor said that one misses everything, the good and the bad; I might also add that one gets used to the good too soon. I was so used to it that one day, because Diana asked me to take her to Ireland Square, I looked at her without hiding my surprise. I was about to scold her when I reconsidered that the missus was always inclined to certain whims and that going to Ireland Square was a most innocent one. I finally gave in. It was Saturday, I remember it well.

While we strolled around the square, I couldn't help wondering: Why did she insist on coming? She hardly talked, she seemed worried. In the hopes of amusing her, I said we should go over to the puppet show. There something really unpleasant awaited me. The comedy took place in an insane asylum and the doctor was horsewhipping a madman. I was afraid Diana would remember her recent confinement and that she would become even more melancholy. I was quite wrong. She laughed, clapped her hands, like a delighted child. When we left, moving her head she commented:

"What fun."

Perhaps because I'm always anxious, I was now waking up every morning worrying about what the day might bring me; what it brought me was the confirmation that things were going well. Diana rarely went out; to go shopping or to walk the dog, she'd ask me to go with her.

One afternoon Professor Standle stopped by. The missus treated him with an indifference that astounded me and she cut him off when he started to put us to a complete test on the technique of training dogs. The big bore, who loves to prolong his visits, said good-bye after a few minutes and, with confusion painted all over his face, left in haste.

It was remarkable how well the two Dianas got along. They didn't need words; they'd look into each other's eyes and you could swear that one knew what the other was thinking. Sometimes I even wondered if they weren't so favorably disposed because they both had the same name. I congratulated myself for buying the dog, because even our most ignorant neighbors repeated that her presence had contributed to the missus' readaptation to home life.

XXXVII

One morning I was having *maté* with Ceferina, when Diana came in and uttered in the most matter-of-fact way these words: "I don't know what's the matter with my watch. It stops every few minutes. You're going to have to take it to a watchmaker."

Ceferina, instead of pouring the water into the *maté* gourd, spilled it over my hand. Out of hurt pride, or because of my burned hand, I got angry.

"To a watchmaker? That's wonderful, and what do you think I'm here for?"

For the first time since she came home I spoke to her in a bad temper.

I went into the shop with the little watch, a very solid appliance, a Cóncer that I bought her last year for Christmas, on José Evaristo Uriburu Street.

After a while Ceferina came in and said to me, "You were always a good worker."

"What do you mean by that?" I asked her.

"That you remind me of those nice boys who are shining examples until the first skirt catches their eye. I'm sure you're behind on your work. What will the customers think?"

"Everyone takes a vacation once in a while."

"One question: if you liked Diana so much, why do you like her now? She's changed. Just think, since she's come back she hasn't even gotten a sore on her lip."

Don't think she was joking.

I thought that Dr. Reger Samaniego was right to warn me against the temptation of pushing Diana back to her old habits. Although the temptation didn't come from me, I had to stay alert so as not to give in to the innuendos of those around me. The doctor's recommendation, which I learned by heart, was at the moment a true support.

"Tell me frankly," I asked Ceferina, "don't you think you're going a bit too far with the missus? You're getting too worked up."

"I don't get worked up over your missus."

The things you have to put up with. Ceferina immediately got into one of those moods of hers.

On the other hand, Diana began the truly arduous task

of getting the family to visit us again. You won't believe it: Adriana María told her that she was under no obligation to put up with me because she wasn't married to me, and if Diana wanted to see her, nobody was going to close the door on her in her father's house.

Don Martín was persuaded, probably attracted by the prospect of a lunch prepared by Diana. How was the poor man to suspect that now it was Ceferina who did the cooking at home? He came the following day. According to Diana, the old man and I looked at each other so sullenly and distrustfully that she wondered if she hadn't ruined all possibility of reconciliation, out of impatience. On this point I must admit that in the mental hospital the missus must have learned to hide her moods — which can be useful — because far from seeming anxious, she started to laugh and said in an irresistibly affectionate tone:

"You look like two dogs who can't decide whether to play or fight. Papa, you must forgive him, because he did it for my good."

Don Martín wouldn't give in, but finally said, "I forgive him if he promises never to put you away again."

"It isn't going to be necessary," Diana asserted with the greatest conviction.

Effusively embracing Don Martín, I repeated, "I promise, I promise."

In spite of his cold and distrustful character, Don Martín couldn't help noticing my sincerity. We moved into the dining room. The meal afforded him a considerable disappointment, but when we feared the worst, he asked for my slippers and we breathed easier. We ended the evening toasting with cider. Old Ceferina, who came in from time to time and looked at us scornfully, ruined a little, at least for me, those moments of family conviviality.

XXXVIII

We were so busy with the simple events of everyday life—rather, with the happiness of being together—that I swear I completely forgot about the seventeenth, which is our anniversary. After dinner one night, goodness knows how, I remembered the date and right then and there I got up the courage to confess my neglect. Courage, every once in a while, receives its rewards. You'll never guess what Diana said.

"I forgot it too. If people love each other all days are equal."

"Equally important," I said, articulating slowly and contentedly.

I looked at Ceferina; she stood there with her mouth open. After a while Diana went to bed. I asked the old woman, "What do you think of that?"

"That she talks like a school teacher."

"Don't be nasty. Before, she surely would have made a scene."

"Probably," she said, pressing her lips together.

"You're not going to deny that she's changed since she came back from the mental hospital."

The old woman smiled in her most unpleasant manner and walked away.

I will always have the consolation of thinking that through the ups and downs of these recent times invariably I felt close to Diana.

XXXIX

On Saturday I wondered with some remorse if Diana wouldn't suddenly ask me to take her to Ireland Square. At siesta time, when I was least expecting it, she made the request, which I heard with a feeling quite close to sadness. I, of course, agreed to her wish and at twilight we reached the square and walked around for about forty minutes in silence.

Reger undoubtedly knew what he was talking about when he indicated to me the need to resist the temptation of pushing Diana back to her old ways. As if suggesting something tremendous and for no particular reason, Ceferina would say to me, "Do you think they did a good job at the mental hospital? I'm not sure that I prefer her changed." In former times, when the missus had a bad temper and was a bit of a wanderer, the old woman's gloating bothered me; now it seemed excessively unfair. That same Saturday I confronted her straightforwardly and told her what I thought.

"Let's try an experiment," she answered.

She clutched the telephone and dialed the number. I looked at her without understanding until indignation led me to protest angrily. And with good reason. The old woman was calling up Adriana María and was inviting her in my name to come to lunch with us on Sunday, with Martincito and the neighbor's little boy.

"How am I going to invite a woman who has insulted and slandered me without justification?"

She paid no attention. As if the person protesting were a boy or a madman, in a severe tone she also advised me, "Don't you even by mistake tell your little wife about tomorrow's luncheon."

Without letting her intimidate me, I answered, "And

you call the family and tell them that the luncheon has been canceled."

I was resolute because I felt sure of my reasons.

She asked, "May I know why?"

"What do you mean why? You don't even remember today's date."

"You're right," she said. "Tomorrow is the twenty-third and the next day is Christmas Eve."

"Which means that because of a whim of yours we're going to have to put up with the family two days in a row."

"We'll have to wait out the storm," she said. "We can't back out now."

Ceferina was also resolute. I admitted to myself that we couldn't back out, but the plan of spending Sunday and Monday nights with the family seemed equally impossible.

That night, while trying to sleep, I made a discovery which startled me. I said to myself that my distrust of doctors was unfair, that Reger's recommendations were reasonable, and that I would never again doubt his good intentions. I hadn't finished this thought when I twitched like someone who's been pricked.

More asleep than awake, Diana asked, "Anything wrong?"

"Nothing," I answered.

I couldn't explain to her that in that moment I had discovered the pale face which spied on me the other night at the shop window was Reger Samaniego's.

XL

The next morning Diana asked me how I had slept. I told her that I had spent the night awake.

"Tonight you're going to sleep," she assured me.

I looked at her, thought she was prettier and also nicer now than anyone, and I decided not to pay any attention to other people. Ceferina is always inventing reasons to be anxious, I said to myself. If we lived alone, Diana and I would be happy. After a while we got up and went to have *maté*. In a sweet little voice which put me on guard, Ceferina spoke to the missus.

"Since it's Sunday I invited your father and your sister. They're going to bring the child. Why don't you show off and make your famous corn pies for lunch?"

Obviously depressed, Diana complained, "I don't feel like cooking today."

I remember that I thought, An indisputable proof of how Ceferina disturbs her.

The old woman insisted, "We must celebrate now that you're all friends again."

"We shouldn't make a big deal about it."

They continued the debate in a friendly tone, until the old woman tilted her head to one side and said deliberately, "Remember, for you every day is a celebration."

Believe me, Diana looked like a poor schoolgirl whom the teacher was calling up to the blackboard to test her on a lesson she didn't know. In the midst of her confusion, she had an idea which made us laugh.

"Are you coming, Lucho?" she said to me. "Let's buy the dough and a can of corn."

You're not going to deny that the idea was funny, especially in the mouth of a cook who is so particular and vain about the dishes she makes. What was happening? The homemaker who always demanded from the green-grocer the freshest corn, was now settling for buying it canned? Still more incredible: a cook, so proud of the lightness and unmistakable stamp of apparent excellence which she achieved in pies, *empanadas*, and other pastries, was going to buy the dough in a pasta factory?

XLI

Very sure of herself, the old woman ordered the missus, "Get a pencil and paper."

Diana followed the order and, with a meekness that would take your breath away, took down the dictation of the list of things we were to buy. I said to myself that in time, when Diana was no longer affected by her memory of the hospital, I would ask her how they managed to bend her character like that.

Before going out, I advised the old woman, "Keep your eye on the dog. We don't want them to steal her."

"They're not going to steal her while she's with me," she answered. "What do you think? We all protect what we love," she added, looking me in the eye as if I could understand her. I didn't understand a thing.

I commented to the missus that the dog had conquered everyone's affection. When we got to the grocery store on the corner of Acha Street, Picardo appeared. The poor fool, who looked so spruced up, passed us by without saying hello.

"What's with him?" I asked.

"Who?"

"Picardo. He didn't say hello."

We then did the shopping. Seeing Diana scrupulously

crossing out the things on the list that had been dictated to her, I couldn't help wondering if the old woman had given her the evil eye. Then I remembered the doctor's recommendations and again I admitted that he was perceptive. We entered the alley and at the other end I glimpsed the old woman in front of the door. When we got there, she raised her arms up high and announced,

"Aldini came to tell you that they've put Elvira away in the mental hospital."

"Impossible," I managed to exclaim.

Squinting her eyes, Ceferina looked at Diana and commented, "We'll see in what shape they bring her back."

I was so disturbed that I couldn't say a word. Finally I said, "I'm going over to Aldini's."

Diana hugged me and murmured in my ear, "Don't go. I don't want to be alone with this witch."

"I'm going and coming right back," I explained.

"Take me."

"I can't."

Really sad or frightened, she begged me, "Don't stay long."

XLII

Aldini was in the backyard, sitting on the end of a long pinewood bench, with his *maté* gourd in his hand, the kettle next to him, and Naughty Boy at his feet. When he saw me he raised an arm as well as he could, slowly moved it around him, and said, "Pardon the mess. This backyard is a pandemonium. When the missus is away, a man lives like a real pig. Imagine, Naughty Boy, who never does, made a mess inside."

"What happened?" I asked.

"What do you think's going to happen?" he answered. "Disorder and dirt pile up. Have a seat."

I sat on the other end of the bench. The old man, who usually displays an intelligence far superior to mine, seemed remarkably diminished that morning. It must be what Don Martín says, that sadness humbles the brain. I raised my voice so that he'd understand.

"I'm asking you what happened to Elvira."

"What can I tell you?" he answered. "She had to be put away."

He arduously passed me the *mate*. I meditated while I drank and then I dared to ask:

"You don't think they're preying on our wives?"

"Preying...?" he repeated, staring at the foam.

I explained in a slightly sarcastic and smug tone, which I myself considered unpleasant.

"Maybe, you know, we're their customers."

Perhaps unfairly I was forgetting the pleasant surprise that, at the time, the bill from the mental hospital had afforded me and I was falling back into my old aversion to the doctor.

"No, no," Aldini protested, to sorrowfully add, "Lately poor Elvira hasn't been herself."

Now it was my turn to make an effort to understand.

"Not herself?" I repeated.

"I don't know what was the matter. She wasn't the same," he said.

Meanwhile, I drank a little brew and thought things over.

"Why didn't you call me?" I asked.

"I didn't see you. You go out very little since Diana came back, and always with her. If you've finally found what they call happiness, I'm not going to be the one to ruin it for you with sadness."

"They'll bring Elvira back to you soon," I said.

"It'll be awhile."

"I also went through an endless wait, but one day they brought her back to me."

"Changed?" he asked in a faint voice. "Changed for the better?"

In a firm tone I answered, "Changed."

"I hope I'll have the same luck."

"You will."

One could see that poor Aldini was too sad for words to pick up his spirits, no matter how right they were. We drank in silence and, as I didn't know what to say to him, I prolonged the visit excessively. Finally I got up.

"When you need me," I said, "call me. I really mean it."

He looked at me anxiously, as if my leaving surprised him. Although I was full of regrets, because it was undeniable that in recent weeks I had completely neglected him, I went home.

How times have changed. Before, in the alley, you would think you were living in the country; it was so quiet, you couldn't even hear the birds. That Sunday, because it was Christmas Eve, when you weren't getting out of the way of firecrackers, you were being deafened by fireworks. I don't know what got into the children in the neighborhood, but I swear, more than a holiday it seemed like the world war. The first victim was the dog who out of fear wouldn't come out from under the bed.

The missus wasn't in the kitchen. Before I could ask for her, Ceferina said, "She couldn't do anything right, so I sent her up to get dressed."

I started thinking about Aldini again. I said, "You won't believe me. If I remembered Aldini once in the last week, it's a lot."

"Love and friendship don't go together," the old woman uttered. "When one is at its peak, the other is down."

And she has the cheek to say that Diana talks like a

school teacher. So as not to begin a new fight, I went straight to the door.

"You're going?" she asked.

"To get dressed," I answered.

There are people who always have on hand some extra irritation. I'll bet you don't know what Ceferina's comment was?

"The master gets angry when I invite his sister-in-law, but when she comes he gets all dolled up."

I controlled myself a second time. Behind my back, the old woman muttered quite loudly, "Men are like dogs."

Confused, I wondered if my love for Diana was enough to make Ceferina hate me.

XLIII

I recall those last days with true apprehension. They reappear in my mind enveloped in a strange light, as if they were views or paintings of a nightmare in progress where the whole world, the children and the people I bear closest to my heart, suddenly pursue some incredibly evil design. I don't ask you to give face value to my interpretations, which could be the digressions of a muddled head, but I swear that in my narration of the events I place great attention on accuracy. Please remember that this is a watchmaker who's writing to you.

The first argument—in which those of us from the house remained mere spectators—occurred when Adriana María forbade the kids to go out on the street.

"You forget that they're boys and not young ladies," Don Martín complained. "Normal boys express themselves by setting off firecrackers, ripping open cats' bellies, and fist-fighting."

They argued at great length. In my heart of hearts I thought Adriana María was right, but I wanted Don Martín to win so that we could be free, at least for a while, from Martincito and his friend.

The overall jittery atmosphere was aggravated by the continuous but always disconcerting bursts of fireworks in the alley and all around the neighborhood.

As it usually happens at tea time, the tension eased off and there was even laughter. The cause of that hilarity was too unpleasant. But let's take one thing at a time, as my father-in-law always lectures. Lunch and siesta time not only dragged on considerably, but they were also what you might call lively.

"Only a spiteful man wouldn't forgive a child," my sister-in-law sprang on me, I no longer know when.

Perhaps she was right but, believe you me, Martincito and his friend, a pale-faced fat boy, drove us all crazy, Diana in particular, which upset me, and also her name-sake, the poor dog who spent the whole damn day with her tail between her legs. I remember that Diana came over to tell me in a whisper:

"I'm going to get an aspirin, I can't stand it another second."

I must admit that Don Martin was impervious. He was the great captain on the commander's bridge, deaf to the crew's privations. Because he was following a TV series that obviously interested him, he didn't even take his eyes off the screen to step out of one of my slippers, grab the fat boy by the back of the neck, and whip him as furiously as if he were the rug.

"*Ave María,* what a way to treat a guest," my sister-in-law protested. "If a neighbor comes to me with complaints tomorrow, I'll tell her to talk to you."

As for me, I defended my father-in-law, because the kids were playing hide-and-seek behind the curtain or under the table and were continually surprising us, without giving us a chance to wonder which was which.

I went to the room to see what was happening with the missus, who hadn't returned. I found her lying on the bed with a wet handkerchief on her forehead.

"Poor Lucho," she said. "How you must love me, to put up with this family."

I thanked her for her kindness, looked into her eyes for a long time, and kissed her. Holding each other close, we returned to the party, like two Christians to the lions. The confusion reached its peak when Adriana María asked her sister to take Martincito into the kitchen for a glass of milk. To everyone's amazement, Diana came out with the fat boy. All of us, believe me, even Don Martín, broke into laughter. Poor Diana blushed and covered her face with her hands; I was afraid that she would start crying right then and there. To make things worse, the old woman commented:

"Now she doesn't recognize the nephew she loves so much."

Fortunately my father-in-law didn't like that little remark at all and snorting with rage he said, "Let's take one thing at a time. First you tell me what's the big idea talking that way to my Diana, who just got out of the nut-house?"

These words were perhaps not the most appropriate, but they brought tears to my eyes, because they showed Don Martín to be a staunch supporter of the missus.

Even though it's wrong for me to say so, I swear that if it weren't for her, for her kindness and way with people, we'd have spent the typical family evening; you know, insinuations and quarrels. At some moment, Adriana María, in a sugary voice, asked me for the genealogical tree which through an excusable error she called gyncological. Diana listened to her without batting an eyelash, Ceferina uttered insinuations, and Don Martín, who acted as supreme peacemaker, forced us to swallow another TV show. How well the missus must have behaved if Adriana María herself remarked to me on it in an aside (in a smug tone, to be sure, making it understood that she and I had an understanding as if we were accomplices, which always infuriates me). When the family was finally leaving, the missus announced:

"I'll take you to the bus stop."

"What bus stop?" Don Martín protested in that coarse way that's so natural to him. "After this obligatory confinement, the lungs demand fresh air. Let's go to Zapiola Square."

"Good idea," Diana exclaimed. "A nice walk for the dog."

"Poor dog," I said. "With her fear of the fireworks, more than a walk, it'll be a torture."

"She has to go out," the old woman said to me impatiently. "You know perfectly well that in the house she doesn't do a thing."

"We can take her out in the garden," I replied.

"She won't do anything in the garden either, because she's afraid and wants to come back in," the missus answered.

As you see, she's not always against what the old woman says.

"Try to find that tree for the next time," Adriana María asked me. "I put it God knows where, in your bedroom maybe. I'm so dizzy!"

Because I was thinking of matters close to my heart, it took me a while to realize that she was talking about the genealogical tree; I was remembering times, now unimaginable, when the missus didn't go out without filling me with anxieties and misgivings. I thought, I swear, that I shouldn't complain about my luck.

XLIV

When the family left, I mentally reviewed the afternoon, judged it to be a real nightmare and then, remembering a saying very much to Aldini's taste, a pandemonium. Forgive me if the impropriety of that saying bothers you. I use it because it indicates, without extenuating circumstances, the confused and perhaps comic aspect of the events that followed; an aspect which, for me, makes them even sadder.

As the visitors were gone, I went back into the house with a feeling of relief. Ceferina then declared,

"This walk will give me some precious time to look over her belongings."

At first I didn't understand, or couldn't believe; then I formally objected:

"How do you think I could allow such an outrage?"

"What's so bad about it?" she asked.

"What do you mean what's so bad?" I repeated.

To get something she wants she's quite foxy.

"If I don't find anything, I'll be the first to admit it."

I gathered strength from my loyalty and didn't give in an inch. I clearly told her, "Listen, I'm loyal to the missus."

She got mad as if she saw something reprehensible and even ridiculous in my words. Sometimes it seems that it annoys a woman when a man assures her he is loyal to another. Ceferina hid her anger as well as she could, to ask in the sweetest little tone,

"What do you gain by leaving me in doubt?"

Nothing, I said to myself. You'll just tire me out and rattle me with innuendos, or don't I remember how stubborn you can be?

While we dragged out the argument, we went to the

123

room and before I could understand the meaning of her actions, she began searching the closet. When I recovered from my amazement, I shouted at her:

"This is an abuse! I'm not going to allow it! Diana turns her back and nobody respects her!"

"Do you have a lot of faith in her?" she asked, almost affectionately.

"Absolutely," I answered.

"Then why don't you let me continue? I'm the one who's going to look bad."

"I'm not going to allow it," I repeated, because I couldn't think of anything else.

Though you won't believe it, the old woman sometimes confuses me. For example, what she said next seemed to me, for the space of a minute—the decisive minute, unfortunately—unobjectionable.

"If I fail," she stated with great solemnity, "I'll never again say a word against Diana. Why don't you run to the gate for a second? It would be uncomfortable if she suddenly came in."

I ran to the gate, looked out, ran back at full speed. I was so upset that if I didn't control myself I would have said, The coast is clear. I shouted, "Stop it."

"Just a little bit more," she assured me, without losing her poise or interrupting her search.

"Don't you understand that there's nothing there?" I asked her. "Finish up once and for all."

"If I don't find anything, who'll be able to put up with you?"

That pretext struck me as funny; it even flattered me. Then I wondered what the old woman could be looking for so earnestly. Without showing my anxiety, I repeated,

"Finish up once and for all."

"I want to leave everything in order," she said, like a reasonable person. "Why don't you go look again to see if she's coming?"

124

I got mad because she said she was going to put things in order, but then continued turning things upside down. I admit that for my part I was thinking, It would be unpleasant if Diana suddenly appeared. I again ran to the gate. When I returned to the bedroom, Ceferina was waving up high, triumphantly, a photograph. I didn't feel curious, but rather tired and afraid. Afraid, perhaps, that an unthinkable revelation would destroy everything forever.

The old woman was holding the photograph by the corner; she didn't let go of it nor did she let me see it. Finally she showed it to me. It was a girl in a park; a girl about twenty years old, quite pretty, but thin and, I would say, sad. I stood there looking at her with a kind of fascination that I myself couldn't seem to explain. Finally I reacted and asked,

"What's wrong with that?"

"What do you mean what's wrong with that?"

"Naturally," I said, "if it were a guy you'd be happy."

I must have hit her in a very sensitive spot, because she opened her mouth and closed it again without saying a word. She recovered too soon.

"Did she mention anything about the girl to you?" she asked. "Not to me."

"Why would she talk about everybody? Maybe it's a friend from the mental hospital and she doesn't mention her out of delicacy or respect which you can't understand. Or she simply doesn't want to remember those days."

I think I won a point. Ceferina loosened her grip and I took the picture away from her. I saw that the paper was unglued and rolled up at the corner that the old woman had had between her fingers. I carefully unrolled it, spread it out over the cardboard; then I saw the printed inscription: *Souvenir from Ireland Square.* I was a little disconcerted.

We heard the dog barking and—you're not going to

believe it—we looked at each other like two accomplices. Ceferina took the photograph.

"I'll leave it where it was," she stated.

She put it among the clothes and very calmly tidied up the closet. I went out to meet Diana—I'm ashamed to say it—so that the other would have time. Diana brought me a little package.

"For you," she said.

She went to give the dog water. On the way to the kitchen, the old woman appeared with the most offensive, smug look on her face. I showed her the little package and said, "While I consented to your mischief, Diana was buying me a present."

She answered me in a whisper, "We don't know who she is."

XLV

When I opened the little package, I was displeased to find that Diana's present was sleeping pills. I asked her in a shrill voice, "How could you think that I would take these?"

The truth is I don't need sleeping pills and I'm proud of the fact.

She insisted. "Last night you didn't sleep a wink. You have to rest."

I think that then I got angry. I repeated the question. "How could you think that I would take these? I guarantee it, the day they do my autopsy they're not going to find a trace of drugs."

The subject must have interested me, because I continued with my speech in a tone that, if not deliberately hostile, was violent in its passion. Suddenly I noticed that

Diana was very sad. I was ashamed and I too got sad; I would have done anything to make her happy. Her little gift perhaps was not appropriate and her insistence ill-timed, but my guilt was greater: blind with pride, even though I loved her more than anything in the world, I tormented her. Ever since she returned from the institute, I had never spoken to her in that way and before I wouldn't have dared. I begged her forgiveness, admitted I had been rude, began to fondle her, but evidently I wasn't relieving her of her sadness. I remember that while I looked at that sad, lovely face I wondered, as if thinking up an absurd suspicion, What made Diana sadder: my harsh words or simply the fact that I wouldn't take the pills? I was ashamed of this thought, which I considered mean; I said to myself that I was continually receiving proof of Diana's love and that she, at least in recent times, was never stubborn or whimsical.

Ceferina opened the door abruptly and announced:
"Dinner is ready."

As she turned around she mumbled words that I interpreted as, "At least the other one cooked."

I think Diana is afraid of her, because you should have seen how quickly she forgot her sadness. She diligently helped to serve and persisted in trying to revive the conversation. Futile goodwill: we finished the meal in silence.

While the women washed the dishes, I played the farce of reading the newspaper and fighting against drowsiness, which without the slightest need of a pill knocks me flat if I didn't sleep the night before. Nothing escapes the old woman, so that it isn't miraculous that she said:

"You too have become a lazybones. Until Diana came back you were a shining example: when I was going to bed, you were still working on the clocks, and now you don't remember that they exist, day or night. Are you going to live off the missus' love?"

"I believe," I answered, "that even the lowest slave deserves a vacation."

As soon as we were back in the bedroom, Diana became sad again. Not knowing how to revive her, I finally said, "Don't worry, I'll take the pills."

I thought that to save face she'd answer that if I didn't want to take them I shouldn't. As if she feared I would go back on my word, she immediately answered, "I'll get a glass of water."

XLVI

I then remembered stories told a while back by Picardo about fellows who put two or three tablets of some drug in young ladies' coffee, and then export them asleep to Central America. Despite my profound worry, I wondered, in jest, where they'd export me.

You can't imagine how difficult it is to convince another person that you're going to take a medicine and not take it, especially when that other person, though she pretends not to, is watching. I, of course, am not outstanding for my talents as a magician or trickster. The situation I am now describing in passing, lasted longer than was fitting, so that I went to the bathroom with the glass—hurriedly, because Diana was following me— threw the contents down the drain, wet my mouth with water, and said, "It wasn't so bad."

I realize that the missus looked at me distrustfully. What definitely helped me to ease her mind was that I was really overcome with sleep. To convince her even more, I rubbed my eyes and yawned in a pretense that increased my state of drowsiness to the point where I fell asleep, to wake up after a while with a jump that I hurried to cover up. That little game was repeated, and when opening my eyes a little I would invariably find Diana's, looking at me attentively, I would almost say, severely. I know that late at night, maybe because thoughts and dreams get mixed up, things that are odd from every point of view seem possible; the truth is that I was sure that Diana, for some purpose she was hiding from me, wanted me to fall asleep. Some say that it is shameful to be frightened by a woman; I admit that I was afraid. The first symptom was insomnia, very slight for sure, because sleep came over me again. I dreamed wild things, that Diana was going to take advantage of my sleep, that she was not only evil but also false. At moments my fear was so great that it woke me up. In one of those awakenings—don't ask me if it was the third or fourth because I lost count—I didn't find before me the missus' wonderful eyes. I carefully moved my head and even sat up a little in an effort to discover where she was; I remember that I thought I was alone—not with relief, but with anxiety, another anxiety that reminded me of other days—until a noise, like that of a mouse among papers, made me look toward the bureau. There I saw her, looking through my drawers, as Ceferina, hours earlier, had looked through her closet. I swear that at first I thought I was the spectator of a pantomime whose only purpose was to embarrass me. I almost shouted to her that the old woman did it against my will and that she didn't find anything. I held back, because it was enough to look at her to realize that she was seriously searching for something. As much as I reflected and mentally reviewed my belongings, I didn't remember any that would justify such determination. Except the Eibar, I thought. Tell me, what would Diana need a revolver for? To kill Ceferina, I said to myself, because I was ready to find any basis for any nonsense. Then I thought that the old woman couldn't matter that much to her and that she

was doubtlessly looking for the revolver to kill me and in-
herit all my things. Fear leads man into conceiving
shameful thoughts. I was saved from sinking completely
into that infamy because Diana interrupted her work, as
if she'd found what she was looking for. I sat up a little
more and saw that she was studying a piece of paper.
That studying took her an extraordinarily long time; then
she put the paper away in the second drawer of my
bureau. In tidying things up she was as careless as
Ceferina: a bad comparison, because my bureau was
always a mess and Diana keeps her closet in order.

Suddenly, I thought Diana was turning around and I
lay back. My heartbeat was silenced by the approaching
footsteps. Diana leaned over me, I swear she gave me a
kiss on the forehead and pronounced twice the words
"poor thing." Those words worked like a soothing balm,
because they reminded me of my mother. I looked in her
eyes, with my eyelids half-closed, and said to myself that
Diana protected me from all the dangers in the world.
From this feeling of security I passed on to incredible
fears and suspicions. I don't know how or why I got to
wondering who was looking at me out of Diana's eyes.

XLVII

Then the missus went around the bed, raised the
blankets, and with very typical movements of hers that I
know by heart, she lay down; as always she tried first one
side and then the other (once she said to me that we are
all little dogs who can't decide which position to lie in)
and finally she fell asleep. After a while, less out of
curiosity than the desire to kill time, taking all sorts of
precautions so as not to awaken her, I got up and went

over to the bureau. When I opened the second drawer, I was surprised, as is to be expected, to discover that the piece of paper Diana had so anxiously looked for was the family tree. After all, I said to myself, she's an Irala and her resemblance to the rest of the family has to come out in some way. Of course I didn't say this against Diana. My reaction, in the initial moment of the find, was one of tenderness. I felt an impulse to hug her, wake her up, tell her my bad thoughts, and ask her to forgive me. With that purpose I went straight to bed, when against my will I thought of another interpretation of her determination to find the family tree. She wanted to study it, I thought, because she's another person. It's to her advantage to know the family ancestors, to find out, for example, her mother's name. It's all there. After a while, as if I were now certain that this was the right interpretation, I thought, The worst is that the poor thing got herself a family that always finds a pretext to talk about the great-grandparents.

Now in bed I continued brooding until at some moment I wondered if I wasn't raving mad. It would be much more natural for me to think that she remembered the family tree, that she felt like asking me where to find it, and that she looked at me because if I really was asleep, she didn't want to wake me up. I was already yielding to a sensation of relief when I reflected that, long before undertaking the search, she had insisted that I take the pills. Maybe she had insisted on the pills because she thought that I had to sleep well that night. In hospitals and other places where one rubs elbows with the medical profession, people get into the bad habit of taking medicine for any old reason. As for me, maybe I exaggerate my aversion to drugs. All during that endless day I had found refuge only at the missus' side and then, because she bought me sleeping pills, I had started to imagine things and to distrust her. Going over the same matters again and again I finally fell asleep. At around eight, some startling dream, God knows what, awoke me. As soon as I raised my eyelids I found the missus' eyes staring at me, as if she wanted to penetrate a secret of mine. The idea struck me as funny, I was going to tell her that I didn't have any secrets, but suddenly it seemed to me that the secret was in her and I got scared.

XLVIII

As I couldn't stand my nerves any longer, I got up and went to the sink. I stuck my wrists under the cold water for a long time; then I rubbed it on my forehead and the back of my neck. I felt confused, convinced that I couldn't go on like this and I started to wonder if I wouldn't suddenly go to the institute, so that they'd give me any old injection or maybe put me away. I couldn't go on like this.

Maté which, according to what I read in *Argentine World*, makes you nervous, calmed me down. The little attention we give it is enough to keep us busy: we drink it, have it refilled, watch another person sip it. I would say that the roundness of the gourd affords the hand a certain satisfaction — don't ask my why. I was surely pondering over all this so as not to think about what was tormenting me. In part, I achieved that aim.

Diana and Ceferina were commenting on the tiring prospect of having to put up with the Iralas again that night. It was a pleasure to see them in agreement. Listening to her, one would think that Diana had nothing to do with Adriana María and Don Martín. That friendliness continued until the old woman's temper couldn't take it any longer and she started to mortify Diana with suggestions for the menu. She really was provoking her. Diana was as diplomatic as can be. She looked at her watch, asked us to excuse her because it was late, took refuge in the bathroom and started the shower. As for me, I went to the clocks; with my mind free I couldn't stand myself. Now in the shop, in front of the pile of clocks in repair, I admitted in my heart of hearts that lately my sense of responsibility was less exacting. Once Ceferina told me that love and a sense of responsibility toward one's work do not go together; I didn't listen to her because she said it against Diana.

I worked the best I could in the hopes of being the watchmaker I once was, of having recovered my vocation. Suddenly I found myself thinking of the long day ahead. Right now after what's happened it's hard for me to say it: I was afraid of all those hours that had to pass before I could be with Diana, to the point of wishing it to be night already, to be with Adriana María. She at least, I said to myself, is the sister. As if dreaming, I imagined myself hugging her tenderly; I say as if dreaming because my imagination worked on its own and showed me Adriana María holding me in a frankly shameless manner, while I felt sad because people didn't understand me. From that I switched to longing for the missus. I longed for her in a strange way, pushed by curiosity, by a need to observe her better, by the great hope of being wrong, of crying in her arms, of asking her to forgive me, of forgetting everything.

I just don't understand myself. After a while Diana came in and I felt like escaping. Perhaps I can explain myself: when she wasn't there, I presumed that it was enough to look at her to leave my sorrows behind and that my brooding was the pure misbehavior of a man spoiled by his luck; but having her beside me I seemed to see, beyond her expression and her skin, a stranger.

She asked me to go with her to the grocer's and to the

market that was in Ballivián Park that morning, to do the shopping on the list prepared by Ceferina. I said that I was going to comb my hair; I went to the room and put the bottle of pills in my pocket.

We went out. I swear that I was looking at things as if I were remembering them. Or perhaps like a man who's saying good-bye.

At the grocer's the owner wasn't in. His daughter, the cause of our famous argument, waited on us. How do you like the way she's turned out? She's big, beautiful, but waits on the public as if she were doing us a favor. We went to the market and finally passed by the drugstore. Under the pretext of asking Don Francisco if his Roskopf was functioning like clockwork, I took him aside, showed him the little bottle, and asked him if those pills were very strong.

He answered me, "A baby can swallow them without any problem."

I took Diana by the arm and we returned home; when she took the food into the kitchen, the other Diana came out for a walk with me. If anyone saw me he would have thought I was crazy, because I swear I was talking to myself and, if I remember correctly, to the dog to hide the fact. Not only to hide the fact, but also because I feel very close to her. When you come right down to it, she must be the only person I completely trust.

Ceferina came out to the garden and called me.

I ate without an appetite. After lunch I dragged out the conversation as long as I could, even though Ceferina and Diana, as always when they're together, made me jumpy. Finally, Ceferina started to wash the floor and I realized it was siesta time.

For some time now my mood continually changes. I said to myself I had no right to be dissatisfied, because the man who is completely in love with a woman can be considered lucky. I said this to Diana, a little in jest and a little just to talk.

"There must be other women who aren't bad-looking," I explained, "take Adriana María, who's just like you, except she doesn't have your soul."

She started crying. She seemed more beautiful than ever and was extremely affectionate, to the point where I ended up forgetting my apprehensions. Afterward I wanted to sleep, but Diana resumed the conversation. Don't ask me what she said to me, because I didn't listen to her. I grew visibly sad. As out of place as it seems, I felt the remorse of a man who has deceived his wife. I couldn't stand it, I jumped out of bed, washed myself for awhile, and then hastily got dressed.

"Where are you going?" she asked.

"I don't know," I said to her.

I knew; I mean, we knew.

XLIX

On the corner of Acha Street, I met up with Picardo in his new suit. In its worst moments, life is like a play where a few bumpkins always come on repeating the same number. Picardo's consists of stepping into your path when you're in the greatest hurry. This time he had a surprise for me.

"The doctor," he said severely, "is annoyed at you."

"What doctor?"

"What do you mean what doctor? Dr. Rivaroli."

"May I know why Dr. Rivaroli is annoyed at me?"

"Don't play the innocent. You took the missus out of the nuthouse without asking his help. He's hurt."

135

"And you, why are you wearing a new suit? Explain that."

He waved his arms up high as if defending himself from a punishment, stepped back a few yards, and ran off.

I walked quickly too, because I thought it necessary to get there as soon as possible. In the mental hospital Campolongo attended to me. Upon my insistence, he took me into the office and went to get Reger Samaniego. I thought that if Reger came soon I would know how to talk to him so that he wouldn't deny me a complete and sincere explanation. Of course there was a wait. When the doctor came, I was already feeling nervous and I didn't remember the little speech I had prepared.

So that you'll understand me, I will try to give an orderly account of that interview which was quite frantic and confused.

"What brings you here?"

"The desire, the need," I tried to calm myself, "to ask you something of the greatest importance to me."

In his humdrum tone he answered, "Ask. I'm always entirely at the service of my patients."

"I've come to ask you, Doctor, about my Diana. I talk to her, I see her working, I have no complaints, but frankly I can't find her."

He said, "I'm not sure I understand you."

"The one you've returned to me must be very good," I explained, "but, how shall I say, to me she's another person. What have you done to her, Doctor?"

Dr. Samaniego hid his wolf face in his hands, which are large and pale. When he raised his face, not only did he seem tired, but very bored with my being there.

"Try to remember," he said. "I warned you against two dangers, remember? In reality those two dangers are related."

I admitted that I didn't understand.

"I warned you that you were going to miss the neurotic woman who lived with you for years. I gave you my classic example of the milkman's horse."

"That I remember perfectly," I answered, trying to maintain a calm discussion, "but Diana and the milkman's horse are not the same."

I think I hit on a point in my favor.

Then I got entangled in explanations and Samaniego cut me off.

"I also warned you that it was unlikely that you would be healthy enough to deal every day with a normal person. There I reminded you of the example of the rotten fruit."

"Look, Doctor, you're speaking to me through little tales and figures of speech, but I'm telling you what I feel. When Diana looks into my eyes, something very strange comes to my mind."

"Don't ask me to make the missus ill because the husband's ill."

As I'm bullheaded, I insisted.

"No, Doctor, I'm not asking you to do that. Listen to me: there's something strange about Diana. She's another person."

The doctor hid his face in his hands again. Suddenly he stood up, raised his arms, and shouted at me.

"So that you have no doubts, I'm going to suggest a very simple strategy. Take all the fingerprints you want of her. Then tell me if she isn't the same."

"You don't understand me. How could you think I would make a mess of the poor thing's fingers like that?"

"Then, are you convinced?"

"I'm telling you the truth: I am almost convinced that it is useless to talk to you. I have no choice but to talk to her. I'm going to find a way of getting the truth out of her."

Reger had sunk into such a long silence that I

wondered if it wasn't a clear indication that he considered the interview over. Moving like a sleepwalker, he went around the desk and over to the sink. I believe that I suddenly thought I would give myself the pleasure of awakening him from that dreamlike state with some sarcastic words on the treatment they used there. I think that in that moment he jabbed me with the needle and I fell asleep.

L

I woke up in a white room, in a bed with white iron posts; next to me was a lighted lamp on a little white night table. At first I was surprised to find myself in blue pajamas, because mine are all striped. With the greatest calm, as if I were explaining a known fact, I then said the words that revealed my misfortune: "I'm not at home." Facing me was a door and to my right a window. I got up and tried to open first one, then the other; I couldn't.

There were explosions in the street and I thought of how frightened poor Diana my dog would be. When bells, whistles, and sirens went off, I saw that my watch said twelve o'clock sharp. Very discouraged I remembered it was Christmas. A good thing they didn't take my watch off. How could they? I'm not in prison, I reflected. I opened the drawer of the night table; there I found my wallet with all the money inside, my pen and my comb. I was missing, of course, my I.D. I thought, I have to ask for it.

I had slept the whole day. I wondered what was happening at home. I began to worry that Diana and Ceferina were worried about me. I pressed a bell. I wanted to find out if they had phoned them and I became indignant in advance, because I assumed that they hadn't called them. Poor women, by now they must be going berserk because of this doctor.

I was going to press the bell again when an orderly appeared, and then the nurse who had offered me a cup of coffee the day I came to get Diana.

"I'm leaving immediately," I announced, "but first you'll have the courtesy to lend me the telephone. I'm going to call home and my lawyer, Dr. Rivaroli, to bring him up-to-date on this abuse."

I saw that behind the orderly the nurse looked at me pleadingly and shook her head no.

"As a first measure," the orderly explained, "you are going to take this pill."

By the way he held me down I realized that for now it was better to lay aside all demands. As the man fiddled with a tube, I showed better spirits and said to him, "I don't need it. I feel perfectly well."

I thought, With another sedative like today's, tomorrow I won't be worth a thing.

"Then you'll eat something," the man said in a friendly tone. "What do you feel like having?"

I didn't feel like anything, except leaving and going home.

"How would you like a little noodle soup and a steak?" the nurse asked.

They went to get the food. I tried to take advantage of those minutes to assess my position and plan a strategy. It's not easy to think when you find yourself in an alarming situation in which you've never been. Maybe the injection Samaniego gave me was still dulling my brain. On the one hand I felt sincerely indignant; on the other, I managed to understand that once in the hands of the nurses accustomed to dealing with madmen, there was no use rebelling. I think it was then that I had a glimpse of my plan to write to you, except that at first my plan was to write to Aldini. I had the feeling that the nurse was going to help me and the best thing was to seek her approval.

They brought me the tray with soup that had more grease in it than noodles, a steak, and boiled potatoes. To gain time I ate a few pieces of bread.

"I'm not very hungry," I admitted.

"You shouldn't let yourself get weak," the orderly answered.

From behind, the nurse looked at me anxiously and said, "Force yourself to eat a little."

I obeyed her.

"Here are your vitamins," the man stated.

I felt my indignation growing and thought that I couldn't hold back a fit of temper. The woman nodded her head yes. I gave up. The pills were large and smelled bad. As they got stuck in my throat, I had to take another glass of water, which partially spilled over.

"He's still nervous," the orderly explained.

"No," I answered firmly. "It's my lack of practice in taking medicine." Pride got the best of me and I explained, "You're not going to believe this, but I swear, until this day not even what you call an injection has entered this body."

The orderly looked at me coldly and, in a tone which I found unpleasant, said, "We'll soon change all that. Come, we'll take you to the bathroom."

I had to go, be there, and return in his company. About those things, you won't believe it, I am very sensitive and I prefer being alone. I thought, Even if it's only for this, I'll make them trust me, so that they won't be watching me day and night.

"We'll leave you a little water, in case you're thirsty," the woman announced.

"Thanks," I said. "I would like to ask you both a favor. Could either of you, when you remember, please look in my jacket to see if my I.D. is there? I don't like to lose my documents."

"You shouldn't think about that now," the man ordered severely.

"Sleep. Sleep well," the woman advised me gently. "If you can't, call. We'll give you a little pill."

There's nothing you can do with these people, they live in another world; just think of them as Martians. They don't understand us because their customs are not ours. As you can imagine, it was hard for me to resign myself to the idea that I was in that other world. I felt that returning to mine was essential, but I didn't fool myself into hoping that getting out of the mental hospital was an easy matter. Of course if at that time I had accurately measured my difficulties I would have given free rein to my nerves, with consequences I prefer not to imagine.

When will I be back? I haven't the slightest idea. If you want to help me, maybe I'll be back home in a few days.

LI

I was completely awake when the nurse came in the following morning with coffee, but I pretended to be asleep. I think I acted that way vaguely intending to spy on her, without remembering that closed eyes don't see anything. Then an inexplicable thing happened. If you think that I'm lying to you, you haven't read attentively what I've been writing; my story proves, I think, that I tell the truth without worrying if I do it well. Besides, in those circumstances, rather than doing well, I was being surprised and annoyed.

It's time for me to tell you that the nurse left the tray on the table, bent over me to look at me close up, and gave me a kiss.

With even more reason I kept up my act, which went on to include those movements people make when they wake up from a deep sleep. She asked me, "How are you? Did you sleep well?"

The woman listened with sincere interest to my answers. I said to myself that such professional care did not go along with the previous little kiss. In my heart of hearts I'm the suspicious type.

That nurse will not let me lie to you. I finished off breakfast with an appetite that was a pleasure to see. I think she said to me, "You don't know how happy I am to see you eating."

Suddenly I thought, In her friendly way, she's making it seem like I was, or still am, sick and need a doctor.

As if she were reading my thoughts, the nurse said, "I'm on your side. I want to help you. Trust me."

I couldn't believe my ears.

"I take it from what you say," I remarked, "that my situation here is risky, right?"

"They all try to escape," she answered, "but no one succeeds. You should escape, you should."

At that moment I became convinced that it was urgent to write to you. I calmed myself a little and said, "I'm going to ask you a favor. Letter paper."

"Later I'll go to the stationery store and get it for you."

"You'll keep it a secret, right?"

"I already told you, trust me."

I harped on it. "Just so long as you keep it a secret."

"You naughty, distrustful man," she said with a grimace. She looked at me close up.

"It's a letter for a friend," I explained. "Could you take it to him? He doesn't live far from here."

"I'd go to the ends of the earth."

"You don't know what a great favor this is. It's very urgent."

"It's more urgent for you to escape, but I don't see how," she answered.

The orderly came in and said, "Let's go to the bathroom."

LII

When I came back to the room they had made the bed. I couldn't help thinking, I can't complain about the treatment. As long as they keep this up. As you can see, they made me comfortable and I was already forgetting the missus and the fact that I was imprisoned. I asked the man if I should get into bed.

He answered, "Do whatever feels best. Of course, don't tire yourself out."

I didn't ask him how I could tire myself out.

He left. I went to the window and once again discovered that there was no way of opening it. So that the nuts don't throw themselves out, I explained to myself.

I saw that it faced onto a triangular inner courtyard, with a small planter filled with weeds in the middle which formed an even smaller, rather narrow, dark, sad triangle. I was on the fifth floor. Above, there was another row of windows.

The nurse came in with the letter paper.

"I don't know how to thank you," I said.

"If you want, I'll tell you."

"How much do I owe you?" I asked.

There was a knock on the door (which surprised me

143

because they all, until that moment, had entered without knocking). It was Dr. Campolongo. I assured him that I'd slept like a log, that I was perfectly fine, that I had had a delicious breakfast, but I spoke as little as possible. I know myself. Anything upsetting makes my blood pressure rise and I come out with one of those temper tantrums which later cause me trouble. He asked me to tell him what illnesses I'd had. I told him:

"Measles, as a little boy, and silly chicken pox. After that I was always what you'd call a healthy man."

When he left, the nurse came in and warned me, "Write while I'm around, so they won't catch you. If I give the signal—two knocks on the door—you hide the paper under the mattress, okay?"

Although I could have sworn that woman was trying to convince me that I was in prison, I thanked her.

I got down to the task industriously, but I immediately suspected that the matter was too complicated to explain to you in four or five pages. I persevered out of sheer will power.

I had a scare because the nurse came in and appeared at my side without making a sound.

"Is the letter ready yet?" she asked.

"Yes," I answered, "but it came out so muddled that I'm writing another one. I'll have it ready in a half hour."

"You better leave it for later. I'm bringing lunch now."

I ate with a good appetite, a rather inexplicable fact in my situation because I don't like to be watched while I'm eating, and the nurse, leaning against the door, did not take her eyes off me. Then she didn't take the tray away and kept looking. To end that scene, I said the first thing that came to my mind.

"You promise the doctors won't read my letter?"

"I promise."

"It's for that friend to get me out of here," I said, before thinking that perhaps I was being imprudent.

144

I noticed that she had a pointy chin, with a beauty mark on the left side, and it seemed as if her eyes were very shiny.

"I wouldn't involve people on the outside if I were you," she said, "but I'll do what you tell me to. I'm here to serve you, in every way, understand? My name is Paula."

She paused between one sentence and the next, perhaps so that I'd understand better. You're going to laugh. I answered her, "I have an aunt named Paula."

"They call you Lucho, don't they? If nobody's around, call me Honey."

After some hesitation I managed to say, "All right."

She took the things away and said, as if thinking aloud, "If you don't trust in me, you're a goner."

LIII

It took me a half hour's work to finish off the letter to my entire satisfaction. Because Paula didn't come, to kill time I made the mistake of rereading it. It was clearer, but not more convincing than the first one. If someone asks me for help with a letter like that, what would I do? I wondered. I'd throw it in the garbage and think of something else.

Lost in my brooding I stopped at the window. After a while I discovered a fact which I considered very strange. If you paused to look, you'd see people in windows on the first, second, third, fourth and even sixth floor; but nobody on the fifth floor.

When the orderly asked me if I wanted to go to the bathroom, I said yes. As on previous occasions, I didn't see a soul on the way. Because my intelligence worked at a great speed that day, I linked one observation with the other and making myself sound like someone talking for the sake of talking I asked, "Isn't there anybody on the fifth floor?"

Because I took him by surprise, he stammered, "No... no." He immediately added, "You."

He left me in the room and went off as if he were in a hurry. After a while Paula came.

"Is the letter ready?" she asked.

"Yes," I said. "I'm going to ask you to take it to this friend."

Moving her lips as if she were chewing sticky candy, Paula read the name and the address.

"Whereabouts is it?" she asked.

"You enter on Acha Street, the second house on the left."

"If I go tonight, will I find him?"

"He's always in," I said, and I asked her another favor. "Take the money, because tomorrow I want more paper, much more. I'm not happy with the letter and tomorrow I'm going to begin again."

"You shouldn't bombard your neighbors. If they think you're crazy, they won't pay any attention."

Because she spoke to me sincerely, I explained, "It's such a strange story that if I write it in four or five pages it seems incredible. Frankly incredible. It's so strange that I'm telling it to someone else to understand it myself."

"They're going to take it wrong," she said to me sadly. "A lot of nuts pass through here and it's not the first time that someone assures me his story is very strange."

I complained, "Listen, Honey, if you think I'm crazy..."

It was only out of fear that I must have spoken to her in such a familiar way. She liked it.

"Sweetie," she said to me, "I'm ready for anything, get it? Tomorrow I'll bring you the paper."

146

"A lot, eh?"

"Yes, a lot; but instead of writing, which isn't good for your health, if I were you I'd rack my brains looking for a way to escape."

LIV

Between the writing, the visits from the nurse, the orderly, Dr. Campolongo, and the meals every few hours, the afternoon went by quickly. At night, in bed, I started thinking.

I made the firm decision to ask Paula to explain to me why it was necessary to escape if I wasn't crazy. What did the doctors gain, after all, by having me locked up? First of all, I'm not a wealthy man; also, as far as I can understand, we're not living in the era of doctors in frock coats and top hats, in Aldini's movie, who steal poor wretches to do experiments. Nowadays, who's going to believe that fable? If I had a calm talk with Samaniego, or even Campolongo, and acted appropriately, they'd surely open the doors wide for me to go home.

It was strange, however, that the nurse, who after all worked at the institute and who must be informed of what was happening there, would insist so much on the need to facilitate my escape. It would be enough to carry that thought a little further, to distrust the nurse and wonder if she weren't an instrument of the doctors. Was she pushing me to escape, so that they would catch me red-handed? It took me some effort to remind myself that I was neither detained nor in prison; a sentence wasn't hanging over me and an attempt to escape was not a crime. Of course they might punish me, give me injections or even electric shock. I was there in the capacity of a sick person, without being sick, and the doctors would let me go when they realized their error. Or did the business consist in putting healthy people away? It was less dangerous to put away sick people who, unfortunately, are never lacking.

I thought that without further delay I should ask Paula to devise a scheme to recover my I.D. I am completely opposed to leaving one's personal documents in strange hands. If they lose it, your claims are worthless, because they don't save you from the agony of going down to the police station on Moreno Street.

I got so nervous over the matter of the I.D. that I couldn't get to sleep. I said to myself that the next day I was going to be tired, that the doctors would notice it, they would give me sedatives, I would sleep and I wouldn't be able to continue my work. Deep down, I was convinced that they'd locked me up never to let me out again.

I suddenly realized that it had been at least twenty-four hours since I'd seriously thought of Diana. Poor thing, she had a fine champion, who, if they lock him up in an insane asylum, can only think about himself.

LV

I was starting to sleep when a dog's barking awakened me. I looked out the window because it had gotten light, and I saw in the courtyard a big dog with stripes like a tiger. I think it's a mastiff.

These doctors can't fool me. To put me at ease, they didn't bother me the first day, but the next morning they began the grand attack. Before coffee, they had already taken some blood samples, even from behind my ear, and with breakfast, in which they did not skimp on bread and jam, they made me swallow large quantities of pills.

Campolongo explained, "They're vitamins."

"I didn't know there were so many kinds," I answered.

"You take them every morning and you'll see what shape we put you in."

"Just like Diana, the missus?"

"Exactly. So that you won't find yourself at a disadvantage. Tell me, Mr. Bordenave, do you ever find, from time to time, how shall I say, that you have some difficulty in reasoning?"

I was stunned. This Dr. Campolongo, after seeing me four or five times, discovered a symptom I thought hidden in the deepest folds of my brain. I found myself before a clinical eye.

"Sometimes I would like to explain myself with greater ease," I said to him. "For example, the other day I wanted to argue with Dr. Samaniego..."

He cut me off abruptly.

"We also have little pills," he explained, "for sluggish thinking."

I informed him, "Yesterday, I was thinking at such a speed all day long, that I myself was amazed."

"Do you want to prevent illness? Are you afraid of treatment?"

"On the contrary, Doctor," I said to him like a hypocrite. "I'm slow, I admit, and I don't believe that you can change a person's nature."

I gathered that I had offended him, because he coldly replied, "We'll do to you what we did to your wife."

He took my blood pressure, listened to my heart and said that it was first-rate. With genuine pride I made him repeat what he had said. He finally left.

I was annoyed, perhaps because of the jabbings or the pills, but especially the conversation. For strategic reasons, so that they wouldn't distrust me, I let myself be treated like a patient. Giving in like that made me sad and angry, as if I had purposely submitted. It seemed to me I was more imprisoned than ever.

Paula brought me a sheaf of paper.

"What's the matter, Sweetie?" she asked. "You look miserable. Instead of all that writing, today take a few pills and you'll sleep like an angel."

I said simply, "What a craze for drugs."

"You have to rest," she insisted. "Always writing. It can't be good for your health."

"Very interesting," I said.

"Don't get angry. I delivered your letter, right into the hands of that friend of yours."

"We'll see what he does," I commented. "Probably nothing, because I sent him a letter that not even I understand. Now I'll start writing again."

"It's dangerous," she said.

"Then, what do you suggest, Nurse? That I take your pills, sleep, and let them do what they want with me?"

"Don't be naughty," she said.

"I'm not naughty," I explained. "You yourself said that I have to escape. Let's see if we can find the way... Meanwhile I'll write a report to Mr. Ramos. Maybe I'll convince him and he'll help me."

Paula thought for me.

"When you write, take out one sheet at a time. You should keep the others permanently under the mattress. At night, I'll take the written pages, so that if they find you out, at least we'll save the ones I keep. Don't mention me, so that they won't separate us."

It's remarkable; when she said that last thing, I believed in the sincerity of her affection. In any case I asked her, "Swear to me that afterward you'll give me back the pages."

"I swear it."

"No matter what?"

"No matter what. I swear. If I can't give them to that friend of yours, I'll give them back to you."

"What do you swear by?"

"By you yourself. By what I love most."

LVI

Before starting to write, I mentally reviewed my last conversation with the doctor. One phrase disturbed me: "We'll do to you what we did to your wife." I said to myself that without waiting for the treatment to really begin — for the moment they were taking blood specimens and building me up with minerals and vitamins — I should escape from the mental institute. Especially, to avoid being filled up with drugs. That point worried me more than the very possibility that they would change me as they did Diana. Can the change be so great? I wondered. Apparently she doesn't notice it. Is it that the old woman, who's such a brooder, has gotten me all steamed up? Let's admit that the change, if there was one, was completely for the better, except in the area of cooking which after all is not the only thing in a great love. I could even add that I've been the one who's benefited the most, because since the missus has been back home she hasn't made me wait up for her anxiously, until God knows what time, not even one night: and that was the nightmare I lived through before they put her away. If I kept that up I would start wondering if Adriana María and the old lady hadn't driven me crazy. I knew they hadn't, but I wanted to think that Diana was the same as ever and that when I returned to her arms I would find happiness.

Suddenly, I said without thinking, as if someone else

were speaking, "One shouldn't be so narrow-minded. Maybe if they fix me up now, I won't see changes in Diana when I go home."

They say I'm bullheaded, but I'm really so reasonable that I began to give in.

LVII

I don't understand a thing. Sometimes it seems that I'm never going to leave here; other times, that I'm going to leave at any moment. If I think that I'm not going to leave, I write feverishly so that you will get me out. If I think that I'm about to leave, I continue writing out of habit. I relive so many memories as the pen rushes along; some are distressing, I don't deny it, but many are pleasant. My opinion is that the final balance is favorable, so that my invariable conviction that I am lucky seems confirmed.

I won't deny to you either that the following morning I awoke with the hope that you would come to get me out. I knew that my letter was too confusing to convince you; but people who are locked up have more than enough time to think of everything, even the wildest hopes. When the nurse came in with breakfast, for a moment I was certain that she was going to tell me: They're coming to get you. As she didn't say anything, I ended up asking her if there was any news. She didn't understand and I explained the question.

Her answer was, "If I were you I wouldn't get my hopes up. You can't imagine the number of people who've been here and who've gone through all that. They all ask us nurses to take a letter to a friend who will come get them out because they're not crazy. Nobody comes."

I asked her, "Nurse, do they lock up people who aren't crazy?"

"How should I know. There are madnesses you can spot a mile away; others, you can't. To these doctors, everybody's crazy. Remember, specialists are very finicky and persistent."

I looked her in the eyes to raise a question I'd been chewing over for some time.

"Now, Nurse, tell me why I should escape."

"Because you're not crazy," she answered.

For me, she made the point perfectly clear. Perhaps I made a mistake by adding, "Then I don't understand the doctor's attitude."

Paula joined her hands together and pleaded with me.

"Don't ask me more," she paused, then she cheered up, spoke quickly, almost cheerfully. "Escape. Find the way; you're more intelligent than I. Once outside I'll tell you everything. When we're snuggled up close to each other."

I replied at once, "I can't be snuggled up close to you."

"And why not?"

"I'm a married man."

"Nowadays, that doesn't matter."

I imagined that she'd be grateful I spoke to her with such total honesty, so I told her, "I love the missus."

What then happened was the absolute end. Maybe I'm wrong to tell it, because Paula is unmarried and because she always helped me. The truth is, the episode affected me so deeply that it got mixed together with nightmares I was going to go through. I still see her, as if in a feverish delirium, when she took off the apron, threw herself on the floor, wallowed to and fro with her arms open wide, all flushed, moaning under her breath, murmuring the most remarkable obscenities, and repeating as if she were calling me, "There's no one on the fifth floor."

"The orderly already told me that," I finally answered.

She stood up very suddenly, buttoned her apron, and smoothed back her messy hair.

"Could you lend me your comb?" she said.

From all that previous congestion and disorder there was no trace other than a tear, which she dried nervously with the back of her hand.

Paula left. Suddenly I said to myself, If there's no one on this floor I should escape. After a while the orderly came and excused himself for being late, because they had kept him busy in surgery. He took me to the bathroom and to the X-ray room, where they took X rays of my head, chest, and back. The nurse didn't even return for lunch. I wondered if I hadn't been too abrupt; of course I wasn't going to let the poor woman think silly things either.

LVIII

My situation was risky. I couldn't give the nurse the wrong idea and I had to recover her good will (which naturally did not seem easy). While I thought about all this I looked at the courtyard below and the dog, the empty windows on the fifth floor, and on the other floors, several characters who were already familiar to me. It's curious how after awhile, any place becomes home to us. I wondered if that happened in prisons, forgetting perhaps that I was finding it out in an insane asylum, which is worse. Actually, the faces I'd see in the windows, though crazy, were not repulsive. There was a man with an ironic smile and good coloring in his face, in a window on the third floor, who greeted me and shrugged his shoulders as if he were saying *Who cares?* There was a long-nosed woman — the only one who was a little unpleasant — who seemed down-hearted; a pale, thin girl with short, frizzy brown hair, in the window right opposite me on the sixth floor, was quite pretty but also must have been very ill, because she chased after something in the air, undoubtedly an imaginary fly, which she crushed furiously between her hands, to then look for it in confusion, first in her palms and finally on the back of her hand; on the fourth floor there was an old man with long hair who, always motionless, perhaps was meditating, but above all an extraordinary calm seemed to flow from him.

You won't believe it: I got used to my neighbors, and once in a while I'd go to the window to see if they were at their posts. They generally were.

I said to myself that I had a lengthy task at hand, that I shouldn't lose more time spying on the neighbors, and I returned to the report. In writing it, I forgot the present situation and put things in their place; I mean that at the center of my great worry was Diana. That's why I took a liking to the work and advanced at the rate of thirty to forty pages a day. The bad thing is that, absorbed in my story, I don't think of escape.

I had faith that everything would come in due time and, to tell the truth, I didn't know how to think of escape because I hadn't gathered the necessary elements to plan it.

After a while, the nurse appeared, all smiley. Her act, I thought, served as a heroic gesture and if she doesn't bear me a grudge we'll be good friends. This was immediately confirmed.

Paula said to me, "Give me your hand."

Then she asked me to close my eyes and I thought the wildest things, that maybe she was going to give me a slip of paper with the name Félix Ramos or, who knows, his visiting card, and that I would then hear, "He's downstairs, waiting." One is always a letdown to people's fantasies. I'll tell it to you as it happened: first I felt the softness and the warmth, and only then did I realize that

Paula had put my hand under her bra. She looked at me as if hopeful.

"Don't reject me," she said seriously. "Don't make me suffer."

I answered her, "I'm not rejecting you, dear..."

If I spoke to her in a familiar way it was out of carelessness. I immediately cut off what I was saying, since I would have enumerated the well-known reasons (I'm married, I love the missus), because I remembered the previous conversation and I thought it better to find a less abruptly final way of saying things. I didn't want to hurt her, but, above all, I didn't want to set her against me, because what mattered was to get out and to get Diana back.

Poor Paula, she managed to interpret my stammer in a way that wouldn't hurt her. She said, "You're thinking that we should be careful. Someone might discover us, separate us, and it would be better to die."

To change the subject, I commented, "What do you say about the dog there in the courtyard?"

"He's for you," she answered.

"I mustn't be the only one in this house who wants to leave," I replied, without letting her speak. "When there's an attempt, the dog barks or attacks."

Paula kept silent, as if she were thinking, Should I or shouldn't I tell him? Finally, she said to me, "Have you prepared the escape plan?"

"When I go to the bathroom, I'll give the orderly a push and lock him in."

"He'll lock you in. No, I thought of a more difficult, but less dangerous, plan. One of these nights I'll bring a tool for you to open the window with."

I think I still hadn't understood.

"The dog will bark at the noise."

"You won't make noise. You'll go along the ledge to the operating room."

156

"That doesn't seem dangerous to you?"

"No, because they won't catch you."

"I'll feel dizzy and the dog, below, will await me with open mouth."

"It doesn't matter. The main thing is for you to escape."

"Which window should I enter by?"

"That one."

She pointed to it. I counted, from left to right, six windows. I said, "Remember to leave it open."

"I'm going to leave it closed, unlocked. We have only one night to do it."

"Tonight?"

"No, no... I'll tell you when. We shouldn't waste it. When you go in the window, you'll see to your right and to your left two little rooms made with metal screens. Listen carefully: don't go into the one on the left. That's where the doctors dress and, if one unfortunately forgot something, they'd come looking for it. In the one on the right there are surgical instruments that are no longer used. There you'll find trousers, a jacket, and shoes that belong to my brother."

"If it's possible," I said to her, "put my I.D. card in a pocket."

"Forget it. Your I.D. is in Samaniego's safebox, out of reach. You can ask for it later when you're free, if you have the nerve."

I couldn't quite swallow the news that I had to resign myself to leaving the I.D., God knows where. It might seem strange to you, but at that stage of the game, the possible misplacement of my I.D. worried me as much as finding myself deprived of freedom. Nevertheless, I'd already been in the insane asylum for two or three days and after an evening in the first precinct I thought myself the unhappiest of men. Of course, the first day is always the hardest. And I'm certainly not going to under-

157

estimate the unpleasantness of renewing a document on Moreno Street. I asked, "When shall we set it for?"

"On the night of the thirty-first, at eleven thirty, you'll take off on your journey along the ledge. At that hour, with the explosions, the dog either won't bark because he's frightened, or they'll think he's barking because of the fireworks and the noisemakers. You wear your watch. Get dressed immediately. At midnight sharp go out into the corridor and through the door on your right you'll go down the spiral staircase. If you're lucky you won't find anybody, because they'll all be drinking cider and toasting in Samaniego's office."

"Thanks," I said to her.

"I'm fat and pesty," she answered, "but I'm also very loving."

LIX

I know that someone once said there's nothing worse than hope. Don't ask me if it was Ceferina, Aldini, or Don Martín. Outside of those three, who else could it be? What matters is that it was the truth. From the moment Paula explained the escape plan to me, I couldn't control myself. The tower of strength, what held me firm and allowed me·to keep waiting, was the writing of this report. Outside of the hours dedicated to work, I lived in anxiety. Not to mention Paula and her advances. A worse danger was not being able to sleep at night and, being nervous, the danger that the orderly or the doctor would notice it and would give me some pills to make me sleep or maybe to break my will. I had to reach the night of the thirty-first in good shape and I had no idea what treatment the doctors had prepared for me. I'd often heard about people who were submitted to rest cures. Let's suppose that they decided to apply that method to me. Believe me: I hurriedly counted the days so that they'd pass quickly.

On the afternoon of the thirty-first I grew more agitated, but I repressed it as well as I could when Campolongo and the orderly visited me. Even in front of Paula I tried to seem calm so that she wouldn't worry and postpone everything for a better moment.

Also, in and around the neighborhood and, as far as I could tell, even beyond the city limits, the noise of fireworks and other pyrotechnics they use to celebrate the end and beginning of each year got louder and louder. The barking also got louder. I remember I made an observation which seemed very appropriate to me. How strange, I said to myself, that dog barks in two tones. I peered out. What two tones am I talking about: two dogs. That's right. The interesting thing is that one of them must have been a hound because of its big ears. I said to myself: An outrage. I'm going to make a complaint. This is not a mental institute, it's a dog kennel.

Here I resume my report to Félix Ramos

At eight Paula arrived with a towel. Under the towel she brought pincers and pliers. I gave her the two pages I had written. She covered them and took them away.

After struggling for a while, I unnailed the window. As the hour drew near, my fear of going out on the ledge and walking along it to the window across the way reached enormous proportions.

The fireworks also increased. On the other hand, the barking from the courtyard diminished until it became plaintive howls. I looked out despondently, because now I only had to go near the window to feel dizzy. The one who was complaining was the mastiff, because his new friend, big ears, was conspicuously absent. For all that I looked I could find only one dog. It's true that there was hardly any light in the courtyard.

159

It seemed that the explosions were all going off at the same time. In those moments I thought of how frightened our poor dog would be, but I said to myself that she was luckier than I, because she was home with the missus.

At a quarter to twelve I closed my eyes and stood outside on the windowsill. I swear, I was forced back into my room no less than four times because of vertigo and fear. I took some steps, feeling for the moldings on the wall that barely jut out. You scratch them uselessly in your urge to grab them, and each time they escape you. Of course, in order not to fall backward you must have the greatest possible will power. When I'd return to the room, my hands would be sweaty and I'd have grains of plaster under my nails. I tried both ways of moving along the ledge: with your back to the void, which seems better for the dizziness because you don't see anything, but which for reasons that I didn't stop to understand prevents you from keeping your balance or makes you even more unbalanced; and facing the void, which is really frightening because it opens before your eyes the complete picture, with the tiles and the planter below, but definitely turns out to be the more acceptable way, because it allows you to get a firm hold and stay pressed against the wall, as long as you don't stiffen up, because then, when you bump against something protruding, you start reeling.

The fifth and last time I went out, when I was halfway there, I started shaking uncontrollably, which was dangerous. Do you know how I overcame that? By an effort of my imagination; it was enough for me to imagine the escape as a street, with the insane asylum on one end and the missus at the other. I continued on my way, which was exhausting because there one doesn't move without risking a fall, and once in a while I stopped to rest. During one of those pauses, I noticed that the pensive-looking long-haired man was not taking his eyes off me for a moment. As long as he doesn't get frightened, scream, and sound the alarm, I thought. Fortunately he remained unflappably serene, as always, and in some way he communicated that feeling to me. The most disagreeable moment was when I had to go around a drainpipe. To rest and calm myself a little, I stopped. I can't tell you how I sweated until the shakes came over me again and I had to think of the two ends of my road, the insane asylum and the missus. After a while I could see that besides the long-haired man I had another spectator: the mastiff. He watched me from below with the greatest attention. When it seemed to me that the tiles of the courtyard and the planter were beginning to move in waves like the water at the beach, I raised my eyes and again sweated profusely; I remembered—because at those moments one thinks of the most unexpected things—that a doctor once told me that in Russian cast-iron foundries foreigners sweated up to eight quarts a day; but that was in the days of the Czars. The sweat that fell from my forehead bothered me and prevented me from seeing. When I wiped my face with my hand I had an extraordinary fright; a little more and I would have fallen. Then, with the greatest care, I started to feel for the pipe. I had to pass it from left to right. First I tried to grasp the pipe above my head with my right hand; happily I realized that on sliding over to the other side that hand would remain behind in a forced position, straining and perhaps dangerous for my balance, which was already shaky; so I grabbed the pipe with my left hand, in a way which if not completely comfortable at first, improved as I passed—of course there was nothing easy about this—to the right side. I swear, I received the greatest surprise of my life. When I succeeded on crossing over the pipe I saw, just for a moment, a smile of approval on the impervious man's face. Although this may seem strange to you, that approval comforted me and

161

from then on I continued my crossing in better spirits. Finally, I was near the sixth window when a thought made me shake again: I had forgotten to remind Paula to leave it open. If it's locked, I thought, to end it once and for all I'll jump. I got there, pushed it, and it opened. I was as happy as if a miracle had taken place and I swear, I lost my balance, to the extent that if I hadn't fallen back I don't know what would have happened. I fell backward, with considerable noise, on to the floor of the room, which was very hard. I lay there, dizzy.

LX

You're going to laugh. I sat on the floor and remained there, God knows how long, with my face in my hands, not so much because of the pain from the fall, which was nothing special, but because of the fright I had on the ledge. I wanted to be near the floor; although I was away from the window, I still felt dizzy standing.

I looked at my watch: it was 12:03. I figure that I must have lost five minutes on futile attempts to go out, so that the endless journey between the windows didn't last more than ten. Although I was only slightly late, I shouldn't delay any further. I examined the room very carefully: in the semi-dark I could make out two little side rooms, which were really no more than corner stands blocked off by chrome-plated screens. With the firm intention of not making a mistake, I mentally reviewed Paula's instructions and entered the little room on the right. I had time to reach for the clothes before they opened the door. I remained motionless with my hand stretched out, and I heard footsteps and the rolling of rubber wheels. They turned the light on. I noticed that I was taller than the screen, so I bent down a little so that they wouldn't see me. I was twisted, uncomfortable, but what frankly upset me was to be off schedule. When the footsteps went away, as nothing interrupted the silence I stretched on tiptoes and over the screen I saw a stretcher with a body completely covered by a sheet, which, because it was short, seemed to be a child's. I thought, Just my luck, they had to bring me a corpse for company. Even if they catch me, I'm not staying. I was getting ready to leave, when I had to bend down because I again heard the rubber wheels and the footsteps. Another corpse. A chain reaction of autopsies, I remember thinking. I'm in the morgue.

I heard the men's voices. The one giving orders was Samaniego. The other, Campolongo, said almost nothing.

Because my cramped position became unbearable, I very cautiously, as if out on the ledge again, stood up straight, half-shielded by a little metal cabinet. Whatever happens, I'll never forget that moment. First of all I saw red stains on the white outfits of the doctors who, when they moved aside, revealed a nightmarish picture: that poor, rather pretty girl, who in the window upstairs chased imaginary flies, lay face down on a stretcher, pale as a corpse, without any sheet to cover her, and there was a round hole in the back of her neck—if I'm not mistaken, at the level of the cerebellum—which was bleeding. Maybe you think I'm a weakling; I closed my eyes, because I was afraid of throwing up, and I leaned on the little cabinet. A little more and I would have pulled it off the wall.

You've got to imagine that those two talked about things, not persons. I remembered stories that went around during my high school years about horrors committed by interns in hospitals.

I tried to understand the situation. The blood flowing from the back of her neck meant that the girl was alive. Why had they brought the other stretcher? Were they going to transplant some organ of the corpse to the girl?

I couldn't believe my ears. Totally matter-of-fact, Samaniego said to Campolongo, "Don't touch the tail."

I held myself back because I realized that if I confronted them in mid-operation, the only victim of my fit of temper would be that poor girl. I managed to ponder, The missus was in the hands of these people.

I was so deeply disturbed that the sound of the wheels and the footsteps moving away startled me. After a while I peered out. They left the stretcher with the dead child, I said to myself. They're going to come back for him.

I had to make a decision: attempt an escape, although things hadn't turned out as Paula had predicted, or take the return trip on the ledge. It was enough to remember the ledge to decide on escape. I put on the trousers and jacket from Paula's brother; so as not to make noise, I would carry the shoes in my hand until I was on the street. The minutes passed and the doctors didn't come back. Since he's dead, they leave him any old place, I thought. I was greatly confused. I persisted in the idea of taking advantage of the midnight toast to escape, though at midnight the doctors had been operating before my very eyes. Add to this, as if it weren't enough, the fact that it was already much later than one o'clock.

I risked everything; I attempted to leave. I advanced a step and stopped to listen so that the fireworks, now less frequent, wouldn't hide some dangerous noise from me. When I passed by the stretcher, simple curiosity led me to raise the sheet. Immediately I received a bite. In a confusion which you can imagine, I saw on the stretcher a hound, struggling to free himself from his bindings. When he barked, I rushed out, for fear that someone would come.

LXI

After a captivity like the one I went through, you don't know what it was to walk freely, at night, along the neighborhood streets. I stopped to gaze at the sky, I looked for the stars that my mother and Ceferina showed me when I was little, the Seven Little Goats, the Three Marías, the Southern Cross, and I said to myself that if it weren't for Paula and my good luck, freedom wouldn't be any closer than them. I turned around to look behind me. I wasn't being followed. On the corner of Lugones Street and the alley, I turned around for the last time and someone grabbed me. When I saw it was Picardo, I wanted to hug him and I almost knocked him down.

"Old boy," I said to him.

He was not friendly in return. He asked, "Did they let you go or did you run away? If they put you away again, don't expect Dr. Rivaroli to get you out. He's disgusted with you and he told me he doesn't care if you rot in there."

I must have been kind of beaten, because instead of answering him as he deserved, I grumbled, "A nice New Year's greeting."

I continued on my way.

"You're not going to get it at home either."

I stopped short because those words alarmed me.

"Can you tell me why?"

"Because nobody's there. Everybody went out. On the town. Do you understand or don't you?"

I understood. I would find the door locked and I didn't have a key, because they confiscated it in the mental hospital, along with my I.D. It was very late. I didn't know if I should to to Aldini's and I didn't want to bother you. I wasn't going to pester my friends at that hour, to ask them the whereabouts of my wife. A legitimate worry, but better not to air. After awhile, I remembered the kitchen window which doesn't close too well.

I got in that way without difficulty. The dog and I embraced like two human beings. I don't know how to explain: I needed little else to make me happy, but that little included the great worry of not knowing where the missus was. I seriously wondered if she hadn't gone back to her old habit of going out at night and I commented bitterly, "Then you won't be able to complain. You'll have her back as she always was."

I looked at the bed to which I so much wanted to return, and I was frightened by the brooding that would begin as soon as I got into it. I even wondered if the best thing wouldn't be to get drunk. Of course not; I had to keep a clear head, just in case they came looking for me from the mental hospital.

As soon as I got into bed and closed my eyes, I glimpsed the saving thought. If it weren't for the confusion that Picardo had left me in—I couldn't quite swallow those words *on the town*—I would have thought of it immediately because it was obvious. I thought, She must be in Don Martín's house. I got up, ran to the telephone, and trembling with hope I dialed the number. There was no answer. Just as I was about to give up, Diana answered. I swear, she couldn't believe it was me.

"Where are you?" she asked.

"At home," I answered.

As if overcome with emotion, it took her a while to speak.

"You escaped?"

"Yes."

There was a silence. Then she said, "How lucky."

I asked, "Should I come to you?"

"They're all asleep," she answered. "You know how

166

they are; they make a big fuss over anything. I'll dress and come over."

"Alone? Don't be crazy. Where's Ceferina?"

"In Martincito's room. She was asleep before twelve. I didn't want her to stay home alone. Want to know something? Since you've been gone we've become great buddies."

"How are you?"

"Fine. A little tired, because I had an endless day."

I didn't have the nerve to tell her I would come get her. If she was tired, I wouldn't keep her up waiting to then bring her back.

"The morning is almost here," I said to her. "We'll be together soon."

I thought that I was spoiled and that there was no reason why I should be disappointed.

The next day soon arrived and I was awakened by the bell, which rang repeatedly. Without thinking that Diana and Ceferina have a key, I said to myself, It's them. It was Samaniego.

LXII

Because I'm a blundering fool, I rushed to the door and met up with the doctor in the garden. For what seemed ages to me we stood facing each other, Samaniego very calm, I determined to do anything, give him a push or call for help. The dog bared her teeth at him. Why deny it, the alley is not the mental hospital and I feel secure here.

As if he were talking to the air, the doctor said, "We've gotten Diana back."

"I don't understand," I said.

"But, friend, you never understand," he answered good-humoredly. "The missus is waiting for you back at the institute, so you'll have no more complaints now. Follow me?"

"Hah, with that tale you're going to lead me to the slaughterhouse? I'll have you know that I'm less of a fool than you think."

"You're reading me wrong," he said. "Why don't you call her?"

"She's at my father-in-law's house."

"She was. Now she's at the institute. Call her."

I went in; he yelled a number at me, but I didn't pay any attention and I looked in the directory. I called, asked for Diana. When I heard her voice it felt like my head was going around in circles.

"A good thing you called," she said. "Come get me."

I swear it was her. Her voice expressed worry and, at the same time, happiness. I defended myself.

"Why don't you come home?"

I felt the impulse to add: I'm not as cowardly as I seem.

Diana answered, "The doctor wants to talk to us. He wants us to set the situation straight, to put an end to the misunderstandings that separate us."

"It so happens the doctor is here."

"I talked to him. He convinced me, but I'll do whatever you two want."

When I turned around, I almost jumped on Samaniego. He was smoking in the armchair with his legs crossed, as comfortable as can be.

"Make yourself at home," I snapped ironically. "One question: what's the big rush to take me back to the mental hospital?"

"To show you the complete file, so that you can make a decision."

"How did you manage to get poor Diana into the conspiracy?"

"Mr. Bordenave, please, tell me frankly: Are you afraid to go to the institute? Do we treat you so badly there?"

Out of sincerity and also because I don't like to complain, I answered, "No, you didn't treat me badly."

"We submitted you to a fortifying rest cure. So, why the fear?"

I didn't know if I should get furious. Convinced of the weight of my argument, I held back and said, "Nobody likes to be locked up."

"Who said you were locked up?"

"It doesn't matter who. The fact is, I was."

"No, sir, you weren't locked up. Besides that, as far as I know, you never showed the slightest desire to leave, to either myself or Dr. Campolongo. If I ask you a question, will you get angry?"

"It depends."

"Were you watching the series on television about those doctors in frock coats, who steal corpses?"

" 'The Secret Shadows.' A friend of mine, Mr. Aldini, watches it."

"Me too, and I discovered something interesting: the fear of doctors always goes hand in hand with a lack of understanding."

"I don't understand," I said.

"In the movie, those diabolical villains with top hats were really honest professionals who stole corpses to know the human body better and save sick people. Do you follow me?"

"I follow you, but what does this have to do with it?"

Samaniego explained.

"For ordinary people in those dark ages, the doctor, especially the researcher, was a sinister character... Well, to children we still are torturers. But you, Bordenave, why do you think we're trying to harm you? Tell me, what do I gain by locking you up? Please, if the things I do don't come out right, don't think I'm evil, but rather a bungler, like everyone else."

With those modest words he got the best of me.

LXIII

As soon as he had me in his office he changed his attitude.

"I want to give you a last chance," he said. He was no longer the friend anxious to help, but the doctor talking to his patient. I started to suspect that I had fallen into a trap.

Samaniego busied himself with an orderly to whom he gave instructions. I looked at the trimming of little heads on the desk, but I was bursting with impatience. When the orderly left, Samaniego closed the door and turned the key. Without being intimidated I said, "See? That I don't like."

He turned the key the other way.

"If you don't like it, I won't lock it," he said. "It's a habit."

"I came with the understanding that I would find the missus here."

"You'll find her," he assured me, "but first let's clear things up so that you, the missus, and I can understand each other."

"Do me a favor and tell me what you have to do with us?" I answered for him, "Nothing."

Samaniego hid his pale face in his also pale and very large hands. When he finally removed them, he commented, "You're always getting angry, Mr. Bordenave. I fear that those temper tantrums keep you from understanding. To everybody's disadvantage, believe me, everybody's."

"It can't be that big a deal. Shall I tell you frankly what I think?"

"Of course."

"I'll bet anything that the missus isn't here."

"But you yourself spoke to her."

"If this is a trap, don't ask me to explain it to you," I answered him. "I'll bet anything that you used Diana as a decoy."

"Will you please follow me?" he said cuttingly.

So as not to appear stubborn I followed him, but uncomfortably. At the end of the corridor there was a door. Samaniego opened it and we went into a little round room and — I couldn't believe it — there was Diana. She was talking on the telephone. As soon as she saw me, she hung up and threw herself in my arms. I was going to ask her whom she was talking to when she said to me:

"I love you. You have to be sure of that. I love you."

I told her that I loved her too. She held me tight and began to cry. Then I was convinced that all my brooding of this recent period had been only madness — the doctor was right, I had been the rotten apple of our marriage — and I decided to improve myself. Without distrust, from now on, I would accept the happiness that Diana wholeheartedly offered me.

"It seems incredible," I said. "I had to go through all this to realize that I'm the luckiest man in the world."

"Thank you," she said to me.

"Let's go home. I promise I won't bother you any more. Let's go right now."

Diana replied, "No, not right now."

"Why not?" I managed to ask.

"Because I know very well that there are things in me

you like and things that you don't like. I've come to suspect that you sometimes have misgivings when you look at me. I swear it's horrible. I love you so much!"

I insisted in good faith, "I promise you that I won't have a relapse of madness again."

Her answer frankly surprised me.

"Maybe it's not madness on your part. Please speak to Dr. Samaniego. You can't imagine how it pains me that there's something in me you reject."

I agreed.

"Let's talk to the doctor."

"The two of you will talk more freely alone. After setting things straight, if you still love me, call me. I'll be waiting."

The doctor asked me, "Shall we return to my office?"

I took Diana's hands, looked into her eyes and said to her, "I'll always love you."

She moved her head, as if she doubted it. I went with Samaniego.

LXIV

"To sum up," the doctor murmured, and opened his arms as if he were saying Mass, "the missus' soul was very ill."

"It is my understanding that science denies the soul's existence."

"Science progresses one step forward and one step back. The soul exists and the body exists, exactly as the old books maintained. Now we have proved it. Medicine found the remedy for some diseases of the body (very few, I know); regarding the diseases of the soul..."

"What are you leading up to?"

"The missus. The missus' present state. Allow me to resume the thread of my argument: these poor sick people, who are commonly called madmen, are practically beaten into a cure. If you don't believe me, why don't you run over to Vieytes Insane Asylum and take a look?"

I answered, "Right now, if you wish."

He smiled amiably, who knows why, and said, "I've searched for new ways of curing."

"Madmen? Are you implying that the missus is crazy?"

"Not at all. A simple disturbance, difficult to cure, of course."

"I don't understand."

"Try to understand, because what I decide will depend upon your answer. Remember, Mr. Bordenave, that a doctor in my specialization is a bit of a police officer and even a judge."

He seemed to be threatening me. I answered, "If you want me to understand, speak clearly."

"Okay. As I was saying, I searched for new cures. I thought: when people sleep, they calm down, and I remembered methods of falling asleep."

"Do they exist?"

"Of course. Just imagine, I had difficulties falling asleep. A man advised me, 'Get into bed in the most comfortable position for you, close your eyes, and imagine that you are walking through a poplar grove. The faster you walk, the faster the trees will pass in the opposite direction. With the movement they'll fade and you will sleep.' The prescription worked until one night the poplars turned into cypress trees and I came out on to a cemetery."

"The cemetery woke you up?"

"Naturally. Another man, the father of a friend, advised me, 'Imagine that you are entering a city. You pass so many streets and so many houses that you finally get tired and fall asleep. In order not to fix your attention on anything, which would be self-defeating, it would be better to have few details and for the city to be empty.' Now, an empty city brings back memories of war movies, of conquered cities, and snipers who ambush you from the houses. At that point you wake up, because you're afraid of an attack."

"And you finally found the right method?" I asked.

"Of course. Without asking anybody, almost, I would say, out of instinct. I imagine a dog, sleeping in the sun, in a raft that floats slowly downstream, on a wide, calm river."

"And then?"

"Then," he answered, "I imagine that I am that dog and I fall asleep."

"That you're the dog?"

"Naturally. Let me warn you that a little barking dog won't do. It has to be a big dog, preferably with a wide head."

I believe that the subject of that conversation calmed me down. It was remarkable: if you saw us, you would have taken us for great friends. Trying to react, I thought, I shouldn't be letting him get me involved and then put me to sleep. I said, "You were going to tell me about your methods for curing certain patients."

"You'll see," he said. "While I searched for ways of falling asleep at night, during the day I searched for ways to cure the soul."

I felt very intelligent when I remarked, "You thought of linking one thing to the other."

"Naturally," he answered. "I was looking for a rest cure, and in some way I realized that for man there was no better rest cure than plunging into animality."

"Now I really don't understand," I said.

He didn't get angry. Things were going so well for me that I feared this conversation was leading to something horrible.

174

LXV

Maybe fear led me to seem so reasonable and friendly. In my sorrow I figured that if I didn't give him pretexts, the doctor wouldn't lock me up. Soon I realized that, if he had a plan, he wouldn't change it even though I played the good boy. I began to get anxious, and when I was about to interrupt him there was a knock at the door. An orderly, or office boy, came in and stood there speaking to him very close up, until Samaniego answered.

"Put the call on intercom."

The orderly left. I didn't know whether to speak or to wait. The telephone rang and I had to sit there. While the doctor talked, I tried to put my thoughts in order, to question him on the missus as soon as he hung up. He greatly startled me when he said, "Don't be afraid. Under no circumstances will you be harmed." He then repeated, "Irreversible, Madam, don't worry. Irreversible." I had a terrible premonition: the woman who spoke to Samaniego was my missus. The doctor was saying that to help me he wasn't going to harm her. As in a nightmare, Diana was against me. Samaniego hung up, sank his face in his hands, to finally look up and ask me with a smile,

"Tell me frankly, Mr. Bordenave: what do you most love about the missus?"

When I heard that question I remembered that sometimes I myself asked it. The coincidence, or whatever it was, made me feel favorably disposed; I overcame my suspicions a little and said sincerely, "The answer is not easy, Doctor. Sometimes I wondered if I didn't love her body above all... but that was before we put her away. Now that you've returned her to me so changed, why should I deny it, I miss the soul that she once had."

Patiently but firmly, he replied, "You'll have to choose."

"I don't understand," I assured him.

"For once it's justifiable," he answered amiably.

Again he covered his face with his hands and kept silent so long that I got impatient. I asked, "Why, Doctor?"

"Remember what Descartes said? How are you going to remember if you never read him. Descartes thought that the soul was in a gland of the brain."

He said a name which sounded like "pineral" or "mineral."

"The missus' soul?" I asked.

He was so annoyed when he answered that he confused me.

"Anybody's soul, my good man. Yours, mine."

"What's the gland called?"

"Forget it, because it doesn't matter and it doesn't even have the function they attributed to it."

"Then why do you mention it?"

"Descartes was not wrong in principle. The soul is in the brain and we can isolate it."

"How do you know?"

"Because we have isolated it," he answered simply.

"Who?"

"That doesn't matter either. The main thing is that we have succeeded in isolating the soul, taking it out if it's ill, curing it outside of the body."

As if I were interested in the explanation, I asked, "Meanwhile, what happens to the body?"

"Without the soul, it doesn't suffer wear, it recovers. I would bet that the missus will never again have those lip sores that bothered her so much."

No, I thought. It can't be. I asked, "Don't tell me that you took out the missus' soul."

"What led us to attempt the experiment was the ab-

176

solute lack of hope in curing her through the usual therapy."

I looked at him carefully, because I suspected that he was making fun of me. He was not making fun. As well as I could, I pronounced the question, "What did you do with her soul?"

"I think that you guessed, Mr. Bordenave. We transferred it to a hound with bluish black and white hair that we chose because of her calm nature, and we kept the body at a low temperature."

Although the terrible meaning of his revelation had not yet penetrated me, I hurried to say, as if I wished to prove to him that I understood perfectly, "You're not going to make me believe that you returned Diana to me."

He put his face in his hands and left it there for the longest moments of my life. He finally moved them aside; his face seemed like that of a corpse.

"With regards to the body, yes."

"With regards to the soul?"

He again came back to life.

"With regards to the soul, Mr. Bordenave, a frankly unforseeable event occurred. As you can understand, in the institute we proceed in accordance with strict standards of judgment."

He pondered so much over his standards of judgment that I got nervous. I asked him, "Why don't you just tell me once and for all what happened to the missus' soul?"

"The missus' soul," he answered, "lodged in a pointer dog with a calm temperament, did not run, within what it is logical to assume, the slightest risk."

I thought he was giving me good news, until something seemed suspicious to me. I asked, "It didn't run the slightest risk, but what happened?"

We did not foresee, we couldn't foresee, that the missus' character would be so restless."

"Okay, you couldn't foresee, but what happened?"

The dog, who was very calm, revealed a certain nervousness."

Believe you me, to get the truth out I had to restrain my nerves and be very insistent. I insisted, "Well, and then?"

"The nervousness increased. Imagine my surprise when a boy who worked at the dog school and who gives us a hand in caring for and feeding the ones we have here (a boy with thick eyebrows, whom you've probably seen around the neighborhood) came with the news that the bitch in question had escaped."

"The bitch in question is my missus," I said in despair.

"She carried the missus' soul," he corrected me. "I swear, we spared no effort to recover her. Of course, when we learned that she had gone into Chas Park, which is a real labyrinth, our hopes flagged, but in no way our determination, believe me, in no way our determination."

I said like a robot, "It seems incredible. A pointer, kind of bluish, in Chas Park. I swear I saw her. Not a minute had passed when the guy with the eyebrows appeared. Incredible."

"Why didn't you hold her?"

"Why was I going to hold her? What did I know? This is a disaster, a real disaster."

"Don't get so upset, Bordenave," he said to me. "Try to calm yourself and to listen until I tell you everything. I have good news."

"It's hard for me to believe," I said. "This is a disaster. I'm in despair."

"Listen to what I'm saying; I don't think you have any reason to be. I did when the dog disappeared. Indeed, I seemed so desperate to Doctor Campolongo one day, that perhaps to suggest a salvation to me, he referred to a case in the Tornú Hospital, where he also works.... A very sick young woman, who could not resign herself to dying and begged all the doctors to save her.... I say to Campolongo, "Our one chance. Why don't you speak to her?" He spoke to her. In less than five minutes the poor girl had accepted. I'll bet you can't guess where the difficulties lay? In the hospital, to get her out. Of course you're not interested in that. We passed her into the missus' body and we left the other body, condemned by disease, to die."

When a man is desperate, he comes out with the strangest questions. I asked, "That person who's inside the missus, how does she know so many details of our life?"

"We instructed her with the elements that we could gather. She's an intelligent, vivacious, very nice girl, I swear."

"Who lived around Ireland Square," I said without thinking.

"How do you know?" he asked.

"That doesn't matter either," I assured him. "What matters is that you changed my Diana."

"You come out winning in every way. I'll admit that the missus' physical beauty is extraordinary. You took her home. You must admit that the missus' soul was diseased and that disease is rarely beautiful. What do you miss, my dear friend? The reproaches, the whims, the deceptions?"

My hands burned with the desire to punch him. I held back, God knows why, and I said to him, "I don't miss the reproaches or the deceptions. Neither do I like disease. I simply love her. I'm going to put an ad in the papers, offering a reward to anyone who returns the pointer."

"It's not necessary," he answered. "We got her back."

LXVI

"Your idea of putting an ad in the paper wasn't bad," the doctor stated. "There are many people ready to move heaven and earth to help those who are suffering because their little dog escaped. The guy with the eyebrows, who knows how to handle these things, wrote the ad and a few days later they brought the dog back."

I almost got up to give him a hug. I murmured, "Why did you take so long to tell me?"

My voice cracked.

"Because if I explain the process to you too hastily, you, who have never heard about these things before, would not understand a thing."

He became silent, as if he had nothing more to say. Because I couldn't find the best way of asking him why he didn't return her to me there and then, I exclaimed, "How nice! So we got Diana back!"

"Her soul. In the meantime, as you must realize, complications set in."

"I don't understand," I said. "Now that we have her, are you going to refuse to give her back to me, Doctor?"

"Not at all. But you must be thoroughly informed of the difficulties we face."

"I'm grateful for all that you did, but why don't you bring her in? I'm dying to see her."

"As she is now?"

Believe you me, that question hit me like a hammer. I barely managed to stutter, "Don't tell me that you're going to bring me the dog."

"No, no," he answered with an assuring smile, "but I see that you're beginning to understand."

Very frightened, I answered, "Believe me, I don't."

180

"Nevertheless, you know that the missus' body is occupied by the girl from Ireland Square."

I couldn't believe my ears.

"If she is, it's your fault," I shouted. "Take her out. Take her out immediately."

He said to me, "Don't ask me to do harm to people. My work loses all its meaning if I make even only one person unhappy."

"Either I'm mistaken or you consider yourself a great benefactor. We'll soon see what people think when they find out."

"At least hear me out before judging. I said that I don't want to make anyone unhappy. That includes you."

"Then all you have to do is to return Diana to me."

"We're getting to that," he said. "Will you allow me an explanation?"

"I consider it useless."

"I don't. I owe you an explanation, though perhaps you don't deserve it. Right here, in the institute, we had an incurable patient who happened to be a beautiful, wonderful girl. I thought..."

"What did you think?"

"Look, I'm telling you she's as pretty as Diana. Even younger, and what delicate features!"

At that point in the discussion I guessed to whom he was referring. Very indignant, I said, "Few women are as pretty as Diana."

"True. It's also true that this girl is very pretty."

"You're not going to compare them."

"First you see her and then we'll talk."

"I've already seen her. You must think I'm an idiot, but I know who you're talking about: the fly chaser."

He opened his mouth and it was his turn to look idiotic, but he recovered too soon.

"You saw the poor thing when she was in very bad

181

shape. Now, with the missus' soul, she's something else. Something else entirely."

"You don't get me, Doctor. I don't want something else. I want Diana."

"Variety's the spice of life," he said.

"You've lost your sense of decency. Didn't they ever tell you that you shouldn't mess around with people like that? I'm telling you. You think you're a great man and you're a common merchant of bodies and souls. A butcher."

"Don't get so worked up," he said to me.

"How do you expect me to be? You told me that you were returning Diana and you tried to pass off a masquerader on me. Didn't you think that it would be horrible to look at one's wife and suspect that a stranger is spying on you from within?"

"That was when you weren't informed. Now you know."

"While you don't even know what a person is. You don't know that if you break her into pieces, you lose her."

I argued with that doctor as if I wanted to convince him. I really only wanted them to give the missus back to me and I was desperate. He said, "With such criteria we couldn't cure diseases or correct shortcomings."

"Didn't you ever realize that one loves people for their shortcomings?" I shouted at him like a wild man. "You're the one who's sick! You're the one who's sick!"

I think it was at that moment that he jabbed me.

LXVII

When I woke up I was back in the little white room. Paula told me to hurry up with the report, because

182

tomorrow they're going to change her floor. When I asked if I could count on her for a new attempt to escape, she answered vaguely. I don't blame her. The poor thing knows what happens to people who go against these doctors.

As Ceferina has told me more than once, my temper tantrums get me into trouble.

I'm sure that the person who spoke on the telephone to Samaniego, while I was in the office, was the girl from Ireland Square. When Samaniego said "Don't worry. It's irreversible," evidently he was promising her that he wouldn't take her out of Diana's body. In any case, if I hadn't gotten angry, maybe I would have persuaded him to pass her into the other girl's body, and to pass the one that belongs to the missus back to her. Maybe it's still not too late.

PART TWO

by

Félix Ramos

Many times in my life I have dreamed of the idea of receiving news that would alter my destiny. This fantasy comes, perhaps, from an undoubtedly false story that I read in some popular magazine, about that desperate, ravenous young Englishman who, on going down to the beach to commit suicide, found a bottle containing the will of the North American magnate Singer, who was leaving his millions to whomever picked it up. One day, at the very door of my house, the dream incredibly turned into reality; but in the version of the story that was destined to me, the romantic elements disappear: there is no bottle, no sea, no will, but rather a pile of papers in a dog's mouth. Our desires are fulfilled in a manner that persuades us that it's much better not to desire anything.

The dog, a tiger-striped mastiff as far as I could tell, unlike the usual mail carriers who month after month leave the magazines I anxiously await in the next door neighbor's entranceway, knew what he was doing. After giving me the envelope he looked at me with determination and, I now believe, with hope. He ran to the door, stood up on his hind legs, leaned on the latch, tried to open it. He couldn't. I suppose that what then occurred was a conflict between his intelligence, extraordinary for an animal, and the reflexes of his species. The reflexes won over, the dog howled. The howls guided the hurried footsteps of a ragamuffin with very bushy eyebrows who works at the dog school on Estomba Street. When the dog saw him, he rapidly attempted a counter-attack and escape. He was restrained without difficulty.

"He escaped," the man explained with a smile that made him more human.

The ragamuffin didn't ask me for the papers.

There's nothing more desolate than the eyes of a sad dog. In those of the poor animal who struggled, almost suffocated, there was desolation, but also reproach. The reproach, I hope I'm wrong, seemed addressed to me.

I went in and examined the file. It contains the signature of the same Lucio Bordenave who had sent me, days ago, through a young lady, a wild and confused letter. After resorting to a dog, what next will my pen pal do to call attention to himself?

For apparently contradictory reasons, I don't have faith in the document's authenticity. First of all, it seems strange that Bordenave would write to me; after all, we've parted ways. It also seems strange that Bordenave addresses me in a formal manner; after all, we've known each other since childhood. The truth is that after reading it, I felt the disappointment of a person who's received an anonymous letter. Or even worse: a letter from an imposter.

I looked up the telephone number of the mental institute on Baigorria Street in the directory, called, and asked for Nurse Paula.

When I told her my name, she asked, "Did you get the papers?"

"Yes. A dog brought them to me."

The woman exclaimed, "Poor little dog! My sweet little dog." She broke into grief-stricken moans and hung up.

Twenty days later, an unpleasant street incident took place right before me. I was rocking in my little wicker armchair in the doorway when Ceferina, a relative of the Bordenaves — a tall, bony, Indian-looking old woman

—came running down the middle of the alley with her hair disheveled and her eyes shining as if she were consumed by fever. She ran until she was in front of me, waving her arms and shouting hysterically:

"The one who came back isn't Lucho! The one who came back isn't Lucho!"

She suddenly collapsed like a rag. I went over to look. She was dead. Soon the curious began to gather around.

I went back into the house, lay down on my bed, tried to forget, and since that was impossible, I did some thinking. I could find only two alternatives: either believe what the report told me, intervene and act like a fool, or not believe, not intervene and act like an egotist.

In order to visit Bordenave that very night, I took advantage of Ceferina's wake, which wasn't a very proper thing to do. Prettier than ever, Diana offered me a cup of coffee and greeted me as if she didn't know me. Lucho looked at me with such impervious indifference that I searched for refuge among a group of friends, among them Fats Picardo, Aldini the Clown, and others whom I could barely recognize, because they had moved and hadn't lived in the alley for years.

Toward dawn, a hullabaloo broke out in the kitchen. I suggested to Picardo, who's a busybody, "Why don't we find out what's happening?" A pale, thin girl with very short hair was shouting at Diana,

"I've come tonight so that the whole neighborhood can hear me! Leave my house! You're an intruder and you know it perfectly well!"

Lucho Bordenave and Mr. Standle, a German, took her by the arms and put her out on the street. When they dragged her away I got closer and I think I saw on the nape of the girl's neck a scar. I think Bordenave had a similar one. Someone said that the German was taking the excited girl to the mental institute. Bordenave's father-in-law Don Martin Irala—an old man in shirtsleeves and slippers — comforted his daughter who seemed very affected by the incident.

The next day I called the institute and asked for Nurse Paula. They asked me, "Who's calling, please?"

"A friend."

"She no longer works with us."

"Could you give me her address?"

"We don't have it. In the room which Mr. Bordenave occupied we found a letter for you. Would you like us to send it to you, Mr. Ramos?"

I said no, because I was tired of Bordenave's letters and because they had recognized me. The whole matter seemed, apart from confusing, threatening. So, I decided to forget about it for awhile.